D0859161

5

BALLAD OF
THE CONFESSOR

Real Literature Tour
Summer 2003

Also by William Zink

The Hole (writing as Marco Polio)
Isle of Man
Torrid Blue
Homage

BALLAD OF THE CONFESSOR

William Zink

Sugar Loaf Press

Alexandria

Copyright © 2003 by William Zink

All rights reserved. No part of this book may be reproduced in any form without written permission from the publisher, except by a reviewer, who may quote brief passages in a review.

The author wishes to thank Lar and Mon, whose support has been unfailing. Also to Jimmy Kelliher for his keen eyes and years of friendship. Finally, to those beautiful laborers, fishermen, and dreamers of the Carolina Low Country; it was my privilege to walk in your shoes.

ISBN 0-9700702-0-9
Library of Congress Control Number: 2002117842

10 9 8 7 6 5 4 3 2 1

Sugar Loaf Press
4160 Raccoon Valley Rd. Alexandria, Ohio 43001
www.sugarloafpress.com

Printed in USA

PROLOGUE

It's the backs of men that move the world. Here at the nursery we move peat, mulch, manure, trees. Elsewhere, they move cast iron, fruit, books, beer, shoes, washers, dryers, stone, brick, coal, cars, houses, cities, philosophies, revolutions, anesthesia. Everything you own was moved by somebody. He moved it in a standing sleep, or daydream, or better yet, fantasy. The fantasies he keeps from his wife or girlfriend because they have not moved the earth all day long, they have no idea. They perceive only the threat and do not see the necessity. The tiniest of *things* have broken men's backs. The pencil of eyeliner or tube of lipstick that you use each morning to ready yourself for the day is an accomplice to psychosis, or perhaps chronic lethargy. The beautiful new hardwood floor in your beautiful new nine hundred square foot great room is a partner in murder. This very book—such an innocuous, common trifle—is the battering ram that broke some poor soul's will to live. Your comfort and convenience—why, your very *existence*—depends upon some laborer's discomfort, or more likely, his misery.

We are the movers of the world! Our fraternity has no volunteers. All were impressed from other ships and lashed to this wheel, the

1

wheel of the invisible, mute beast, purgatory of sweat, blisters, and fatigue. Some know that this will be their station in life. Others believe it is only temporary, are fooled or fool themselves, and later are destroyed when the balloon of self-delusion bursts. For some, it is temporary, and they escape and forever look from the outside-in; but they never forget, even those who attempt to bury it beneath layers of contempt—for contempt is only a Scarlet Letter for one who fears his past, or his future.

Most of the men I know, they aren't going anywhere. They'll remain movers until they are old. If they're lucky they will have attained a higher status, some lowly overseer's position; pointing, directing, heaping misplaced retribution on innocent bodies. These lucky ones might work until suddenly the dim flicker that is their life is blown out by a wind, or is doused by a storm. Most will not be so lucky; they'll labor up to the very end. Their future is a dark tunnel of slow and miserable decay without exit, and without retreat. When hands can no longer grip, when legs become shot with arthritis— knee or hip joints grinding bone against bone, making each step a test of faith—and especially when the back can no longer handle the daily tonnage placed upon it—this man will be discarded, like rotten fruit, and his early demise will be secretly prayed for by neighbors, relatives, and maybe even his wife. Alcohol, very likely, will become his daily companion, his reminder of the capricious nature of his God, or gods, or no God, and it will end pitifully, without mercy, until his heart beats its final beat.

I don't think too far ahead. No, that's not exactly true. I think far, far ahead to the vast and monotonous plain of weariness and its sudden, sacrificial cliff; it's something I can see because it's what I fear most. But I don't think of tomorrow, or next week. The daily collisions with trucks, and trees, and humiliation have ground my once sharp edges. The tonnage has made me who I am and will determine, much more than my intellect or desires, who I will be. I am shaped by the erosive elements of time, like a river, or valley, or tree. I bend when I must bend; I give way layers of myself when I think it will keep the rest of me whole. My limbs become fleshed with muscle. My face is scored with refusals and silent confessions to an ambivalent sun. My eyes watch but my lips seldom give evidence of thoughts which are in constant excitation and then detonate, like popcorn, in my mind. This is my life. This is the life of the movers of the world.

FROM THE CHAOS

Reggie is black. I am white. I make note of this for purposes of visualization, to allow your imagination to fill in gaps, or impose preconceived notions of the cookie cutter variety. Reggie is the boss. Of me, anyway. Ben is the real boss. He's white. I'll bet your mind is whirring with inferences. That's because you're out there looking into this fish bowl. We, within, know better.

Reggie has a compact frame. His muscles come from moving trees, blocks of peat moss, bags of manure. You should see his shoulders. He's solid. I know because when we're unloading trucks he likes to screw with me; he'll pretend to accidentally bump me while I have a tree trunk in each hand, my shoulders being uprooted from their sockets. He's a subtle prankster, Reggie. He never trips me. He just bumps me. He's like a bull on two legs. Even his gut is solid. One day we were on break sitting under the potted trees, and I felt it. It was sticking out like a bowl of raised dough. I thought it would be soft, but when I placed my open hand on it, it was firm, like a big hunk of clay.

"You got somebody in there?" I said.

Reggie just grinned.

"Jesus. You got a hard stomach. Is that from all those potato chips?"

"Huh-uh," Reggie said with a lurch. He answered me seriously. Reggie doesn't joke around too much with his mouth; he uses his body. He stares a lot. I think he thinks a lot, but he's not the gabby type and so it's hard to tell. Some days we'll go both ten-minute breaks and the whole half-hour lunch without saying a word to each other. There's nothing to do but eat, and stare. I stare past Reggie's head, and he stares past my head. It's easy to fall asleep on break. The boss, Ben I mean, doesn't mind as long as your nap doesn't spill into work time. The first time I saw Reggie fall asleep on break I woke him up. I thought he was going to get canned. He got mad.

"What're you *doin'*, boy?" He looked at me all hurtful, as though I just farted in church. "Don't ever wake me when I'm sleeping," he said. He stood up, and walked away shaking his head. Reggie has a watch with a timer on it, and he always sets it first thing when we go on break. If we know we're going to be sleeping, we sit under the potted trees. We sit there when we don't plan on sleeping too because it's shady and private and that's where we hide our worms. The pots are just the right height off the ground. They're full of wood chips that cushion your behind like a pillow. You fold your arms, lean back against a tree trunk, and next thing you know Reggie's watch is chirping like a bluebird. When we're not sleeping or staring past each other's heads, we talk about things. We talk an awful lot about worms.

"How many you get?" I said to him.

"Oh. . . I don' know. A dozen maybe."

"Big ones? You got any really big ones?"

"A few."

"How many?"

"Three," he said, holding up three fingers.

Ballad of the Confessor

"Three? You know how many I got?"

"How many?"

"Eight."

"Eight? Gee."

"Wanna see 'em?"

I reached behind me to where I hid my coffee can and brought it out for him to see. He leaned over and looked inside. His eyes got big with amazement.

"Where'd you find 'em?" he asked me.

"Found 'em when I was moving the azaleas. Man, those roots were grown real thick into the black matting. Worms everywhere."

"Are there any more?"

I shook my head no. "Got 'em all moved. But look. Must have three dozen in there—and eight monsters."

"You going fishing tonight?"

"It's Thursday," I said. "You know I can't fish except on the weekends."

"Tomorrow?"

"Hope to."

"You better put 'em in the ice box."

"I know."

"They'll die out in the heat. Whew!"

"You want some of 'em?"

"Awww. . ."

"Here," I said and offered him the coffee can. He looked inside again, but wouldn't take any.

"No. You keep 'em."

"But I don't think I'll use 'em all. Go ahead."

"I got plenty," he said, jiggling his own can.

"I'll have to let some go," I said.

"Don't tell me where."

"I won't."

"I don't wanna know," he looked away, tossing out his tough, dry hands.

"I'll give some to my neighbor. He's fishing all the time."

"You may as well," Reggie shrugged his shoulders.

"You going fishing tonight after work?"

"Maybe."

"Where?"

"Up the Cooper River."

"Who with?"

"Just me."

"Not with your wife and kids?"

"Naw," he said now with his arms folded. "They go enough."

"Sure you don't want any? You might need some later."

"Don't need 'em."

"Okay," I said and put the can back in the circular depression I'd made for it in the mulch. "What time is it?"

"Twelve-twenty."

"Twelve-twenty? I thought it was twelve-thirty by now."

"Naw, it's only twelve-twenty."

Reggie used to be a sinner. He told me about it one day, just before quitting time. We sat on piled up railroad ties with the sun cutting low and sharp through the trees. My feet were dead. Reggie's words floated through my ears like soft doves, and the creosote smell reminded me of our place in the world.

"I used to be a sinner something awful. I cussed all the time, and smoked that funny stuff. I smoked it constantly; well, every day a little. I was married before I married the wife I have now. We lived in Baltimore. I was a DJ at this club. She was always nagging at me. Nag, nag, nag. One day I'd had enough, so I just left. Didn't never go back. Didn't call to let her know where I was 'til six months later.

Ballad of the Confessor

There she was, nagging at me on the phone. 'Good-bye,' I says to her and hung up. That was the last time I ever talked to her. I came back to Charleston. I was still smoking the funny stuff and messing around with the ladies." Reggie paused. His eyes narrowed and he grinned out one corner of his mouth. "Oh," he said, his voice high and giddy with memories, "those were some times. I was a bad, bad man. Lord, forgive me. Something told me I was doing wrong. Not a voice exactly. Something inside. But I kept smoking, and kept taking advantage of the ladies. I was on a subway to eternal damnation, you better believe it. One day my sister—she's a minister down toward Beaufort—she asked me if I wanted to go to church on Sunday. You see, she asked me every week for three years. I always said no. But this time I said yes. I just said yes, just like that. So," he shrugged, "I went. And then, because I liked it so much, I went the next Sunday. Then the Sunday after that, and the Sunday after that. I haven't missed a Sunday since, and that was over ten years ago. I go two or three times a week. I stopped fooling around and smoking the funny stuff. Now I got a wife and two kids. You never know. Who would've thought I'd be a church-going man? But I am. That's me. The thought of going to church used to make me wanna run and hide. I laughed at people who talked about the Lord. But now I can't wait to get there. It's the piece that was missing in my life."

There's a Baptist church along the highway between our place and the Food Lion. It seems there's always people inside clapping and singing. They stay for hours. Sometimes I wish I was black. I'd walk right down to that Baptist church and join in. I don't think anybody would stop me, even though I'm white, but I'm not the type who likes attention. I wish I could sing; maybe then I'd have an *in*. Sometimes I want to trade places with Reggie or some of the other movers. They wouldn't understand that. They don't realize that lone-liness is the worst thing there is. They might be poor, and they might

8

have a crummy job, but they have what I don't have, and what I'll never have. When I see people walking through the nursery, I try to read their faces. I look for clues, and then expand on the clues and a life emerges, an imagined life, I know, but it seems plausible, and not only plausible, but probable. Loneliness, I have determined, is widespread. It's covered by many things. Wealth, laughter, activity. But it never goes away. Some of the black movers resent me. I can understand them, but they don't understand me. They see my fortune for being white. I see their fortune for being black. You envy what is beyond your grasp. It hammers away at you—it consumes your mind and pushes you into fantasies you shouldn't be having. I'm trapped. No one in his right mind likes being a mover, but I do sometimes. I do, but everything funnels my attention to the outside, and escape. I think vaguely about my real life, the life that's mine outside this nightmarish detour. It's filled with cars, houses, boats, and hammocks. Even those here who resent me, acknowledge me. I belong. Not to the brotherhood of their race, but to the fraternity of all men who sweat, and groan, and wish. This is the great equalizer. Here, respect or no respect is earned by physical exertion. Nobody cares who your daddy is.

We go fishing, me and Reggie. My wife doesn't like him, and his wife doesn't like me. We go just the two of us. He likes the rivers where he can use his skill in casting, but I like the ocean. We were out on Sullivan's Island one day. It was hot. We wear cut-offs so we can walk right into the water whenever we want. I was in the water doing a breaststroke, occasionally going all the way under to cool off my head; Reggie was onshore sitting on his upside-down bucket. He wore a long sleeve shirt unbuttoned, and a straw hat. He's not afraid of the water, but only goes in when he has two big amoeba sweat spots under his arms, and the ridge at the top of his gut is full of warm sweat. He just sort of sits in neck-deep water bobbing up and

Ballad of the Confessor

down like a buoy. It's easy to tell when he's peeing; he doesn't move at all, not even his head, and then he'll swim up shore a little. I float on my back with my arms out, and if the sun's not right overhead I'll open my eyes and look at the clouds bleached white from the brightness, and sometimes I want to die right then and there because nothing feels better. It's hard to know what to do with moments like that. Sometimes you want to preserve them, and other times you want to devour them because you're filled with ecstasy and you feel powerful. It's been my experience that there isn't anything you can do with pockets of ecstasy; it's impossible to even truly enjoy them. People go by. Not too many where we fish. It's funny how a girl in a bathing suit makes the day sparkle. You can watch her, and hold her image in your mind everywhere you go; think about her at dinner, watching TV, let her consume you in bed before you drift off. It's a form of infidelity, I suppose.

Once I drifted way, way out there close to the big buoy with the light on it. Because I was so near, and so far from shore, I swam to it. I climbed up and sat on the faded, round fiberglass surface covered with gull and pelican shit. I shivered until I dried off, and then it was hot and that gave me the courage to dive back in and swim to shore. Just before I dove in I looked into the slate-colored water; it mesmerized me, and I thought about all sorts of wild, dangerous things. I thought about hostilities, and vengeances, and chaos, and for that first instant it was all clear and strangely beautiful; but it quickly faded and became terrifying—the very thing that had seemed beautiful moments before. That's what made me dive, really. Not the courage from the heat, but the fear from the chaos.

RETREAT INTO DARKNESS

I first saw Carl near one of the hotdog stands in the Battery. It was close to noon. He was sitting on the wall that runs along the south side of Broad Street Park watching the skirts go by. I was sitting on the wall too, farther down, watching just like him. The girl working the hotdog stand was a real cutie. Short, blonde, friendly. She had the right combination of exposed, tanned flesh, and darting love-me eyes to keep you coming back. Across the street the Gullah women sat on the cement sidewalk weaving their baskets. Three boys on skateboards with pants down to the middle of their asses moved in between the teeming lunch crowd. A man stood in direct sunlight eating an ice cream cone that was melting down his slim, tanned fingers. He stared at the tops of buildings with a curious, disoriented expression, like a just-returned migratory bird.

The paper from one of Carl's hotdogs blew away. He got up in a rush, and one of his hotdogs fell off his lap and onto the ground. He picked up the hotdog, set it on the ledge, and went after the paper. The paper made quick progress down the street, especially when you consider the globs of mustard and relish pasted to it. He returned with the paper, which was now a yellow and green ball, and pushed it with his thumb into the front pocket of his grubby-looking jeans. He took the hotdog from the ledge, turned it in all directions looking it over, then ate it. When he got up and began walking down the street, I followed him.

The sidewalk was bursting with men of all social strata giving lazy smiles to women in bright dresses or shimmering business suits; all bounce, and jasmine or faint rose smells, taunting you with the closeness of their bound up desires. I wanted to stay and walk among them all day, but Carl turned north, heading to a part of town that the historical society and civic planners had not yet graced with their fiscal magnanimity. Soon there were no more leering men and no more jasmine-scented temptations. They were replaced by the harsh sound of reconstruction: sawing, and pounding, and banging. Half the storefronts were boarded up. The definitive sign of civic abandonment were the Palmetto trees. Here, they were not groomed as they were elsewhere; dead fronds jutted angularly from their pineapple heads, or lay littered about their trunks like ignored carcasses. Suddenly, Carl stopped beneath an awning that had a huge thunderbolt rip in the canvas, at the door of some really dumpy-looking used bookstore. He unlocked the door and flipped the cardboard clock that read *Be back at 11:45* over so it said *OPEN*. It was 12:30.

When I entered his shop he didn't acknowledge my presence—a potential customer no less—with anything more than a nod, squint, and a long drag from his filter-less, suicide cigarettes. The smoke was choking me. There were plenty of windows, but only one was open. He had a cheap plastic fan sitting not a foot away from him on a stack of *Life* magazines blowing air on his face. I began to sweat immediately.

"Got anything on fishes?" I asked him.

He took a long hit from the cigarette. When he did he leaned forward out of the air blast wedge. He looked more like he was eat-

ing than puffing. "I don't know," he said with indifference. "You'll
have to look around. Plants and animals are over there." He pointed
to a corner where the paint on the wall was hanging in long, shag-
bark hickory shreds. I wasn't really looking for a book on fishes. If
I'd been looking for any book at all, it would have been a book on
Colorado. I had been thinking of moving to Colorado for some time.
"How about local stuff? Got anything on Moultrie or Fort Sumter?"

There was no answer. He seemed preoccupied with something in
his lap.

"Hey? How about dinosaurs? Got any dinosaur books?"

Carl moved his head to look between two shelves. "Huh?" he
said cupping his ear. "I can't hear in this ear."

I walked toward him. "I said, do you have any dinosaur books?"

"Dinosaurs?" he said, sneering, like the question pissed him off.

"Yeah, dinosaurs. You know. You got any?"

"What kind of dinosaurs?"

"I don't know what kind. That's why I'm looking for a book," I
said.

"What do you want a book on *dinosaurs* for?" he asked me. "PBS
has a series that's better than any book."

"Really," I said. I was thinking he was about the most sarcastic,
snidest asshole I'd ever met.

"You don't want to buy a book on dinosaurs," he told me, like he
was the dinosaur guru of the whole wide world.

"So you don't have any?"

"Sorry," he said, "but we don't have any *dinosaur* books."

The place stunk. It was a different kind of stench—somewhere
between a heavy mildew and buttered popcorn, armpit smell. Even
for a used bookstore the books looked old and haggard. Dust covered everything. You could see where a book had been removed or
put back, because the coating of dust there was smeared. Cheap

Ballad of the Confessor

pictures hung from the peeling walls. Bad reproductions of Marilyn Monroe, Elvis, L.B.J., Michael Jackson. Small hand written price tags on strings hung from the pictures, and also from the assorted hodge-podge of flea market type junk. The limp price tags looked hopeless. I glanced over at Carl. I watched him. Behind the once-garish counter, now muted, chipped, the front pane slashed with a long, diagonal crack, he sat, smoke rising between stacks of books like it does from morning embers after the fire, his gray face like some relic staring, and thinking.

I strolled past the counter. Behind him were more cheap pictures. But one stood out. It was a jungle scene done on some sort of velvety material. The painting showed a boy, his eyes wide like a le-mur's, looking out from a luscious wall of vegetation. The boy looked frightened and lost with a huge machine gun cocked across his diminutive frame. Though he was an American, the rendition had a decidedly Asian quality to it, especially in the eyes.

"You want something?" Carl said through a long, wincing drag of his cigarette.

"That picture. Can I see it?" I pointed to it.

He turned around. "What, *that*?"

"Yeah. Can I look at it?"

He studied me, then doused the stub of his cigarette in a large glass ashtray completely filled with butts. He removed the painting from the wall, holding it delicately at the edges as though it were something truly valuable. He wouldn't allow me to touch it.

"That's really different," I said. "I've never seen anything like it. Where did you get it?"

"I bought it for my mother," Carl said; his voice took on an un-sentimental softness. It seemed to be hurting him to let me look at the painting. Up close the boy was even smaller, and the machine gun bigger.

14

"How much?"

"For you, two thousand dollars."

I lifted my eyes. "Two thousand dollars?"

"That's right. You got two thousand dollars?"

"Not on me."

"That's what it costs," he said, placing it carefully back up on the wall. "Maybe two thousand five hundred."

I noticed a wedding band on his finger. There was a color photograph of a woman standing with her face resting affectionately against the back of a horse—unframed—leaning behind the massive ashtray. The photograph looked at least twenty years old. It was curled at the edges and sat where he could see it with every flick of ashes, every smashing of butt. The words *Love you, Carl Elise* were written in the lower left corner in black marker. I decided to leave. As I was walking past him he was finishing up a bite-puff of his cigarette; he looked up all sheepish, as though he'd been caught doing something. His hair was a mass of flattened gray-black curls. His face was dark from the sun, his eyes were pulled by massive, puffy half-rings below. "Take it easy," he said. I walked out.

The next time I saw Carl was a few months later. I was downtown walking the streets. It was maybe 10:30, not very late. The air was thick with sea sludge smells, and a cigar from a man walking ahead of me. I was heading toward East Bay, walking through the park, when I heard a cough. The sound startled me. The park at night is eerie enough with its deep shadows, Palmetto bugs, and the occasional lumbering rat. I slowed without stopping, and moved my eyes in the direction of the cough. There was nothing but the deep recesses of shadow formed by the Polaroid-like freeze-frames of shrubbery and low tree branches. I feared something would burst out at me from the darkness. You could see eyes, claws, or fangs—everything—it was all there, if you lingered on your fears. While still searching the bushes with my eyes, I plotted my escape. I remembered I had a pack of gum in my pocket. I stopped and fished it out in a spontaneous diversionary tactic. I unwrapped it, listening, looking into the dark corner of the park. My heart beat fast. My muscles tensed involuntarily.

"Hey, I know you're over there," I said, and after I'd said it I thought I shouldn't have. I put the piece of gum in my mouth and now because I'd called over I looked into the darkness openly, my eyes not in focus on any specific object but staying ready for sudden movement. There was nothing. I waited. I knew that unless I went over and searched behind the tree trunks and bushes, I wouldn't find him. Piss on that. "Fine," I said. I turned then, and headed up the long cement walkway toward the street, and soon I was out of the park and beneath the poet's night-blur of streetlights. I went on toward East Bay when a thought occurred to me—it came fast—I acted on it without giving myself a chance to back out. I headed back toward the park. But instead of going in the way I'd just left, I went around the block back to where I originally went in. I moved quickly—in a brisk Gestapo walk, then broke into a full run—passing closed shop fronts. As I ran I looked into the windows, the way I did as a youth running through the streets of town. But when I saw my reflection I jerked my head back—it felt like a thumb pushing on my eyes. I suddenly felt foolish. And yet, that's what kept me going—it was as though I were stepping outside myself, through a hole, into a world that couldn't be made safe or predictable. It was the most thrilling feeling I could remember and it gave me courage and made me feel that what I was doing was essential and predetermined and somehow sanctified. The wind moved the beads of sweat on my face, and teased my hair into insubordinate dances away from my temple. I felt like a passenger without control.

I stopped, making myself flat against the office building at the side entrance to the park. As I rounded the corner I slid down into a crouch, then slumped forward to my hands and knees. I crawled between the office building and the thick tentacles of magnolia, and the sharp jab of boxwood and hibiscus. I moved without sound, or so I thought, straining my neck, peering into the slowly emerging geometric shadows.

"Stop right there," came a voice from up ahead. It was a desperate, high-octave voice.

"Hello?" I lifted my head. "Hello?" There were only the dark pockets of shadow.

"Stop!" the jittery voice cried out.

"All right!" I shouted back. The voice, and therefore the man behind it, was no more than ten feet away. I eased back off my hands and knees to a crouch. "Where are you? I can't see you—"

"What do you want? I have a knife!"

"Nothing," I said. "Don't worry. I'm a friend."

"Who are you?"

"Can you see me? I can't see you. Come out in the light."

"I'm not going anywhere. You some kind of faggot?"

"No."

"You sure?"

"Sure I'm sure."

"If that's what you have in mind. . . you better not—I have a knife!"

"Listen. I don't want anything—"

"Then why are you here? Why did you sneak back here? What do you want!"

I didn't know what to say. In that brief moment, I looked inside myself and couldn't find an answer. And because I couldn't find an answer, the question doused me like a bucket of water.

"I'm like you," I blurted out.

Ballad of the Confessor

"Like me? You don't know who I am."

"That's true. I know. You're right."

"Then why do you say you're like me?"

"You're here, on the ground, in this park. And so am I."

"Is that what you want? You looking for a place to sleep? Bullshit. Bullshit."

"No, I'm not looking for a place to sleep. No, listen; I was just passing through on my way to my car—and I heard you. It surprised me. I became curious. I can't explain it. I'm a little drunk, and it's hot. I want to get home and take a shower. I have to get this grime off of me. It's the shadows. The streetlights. The windows with my reflection—there, there, and there! The sidewalks are alive, man! I don't know. I just don't know."

Inexplicably, I felt the urge to rip out of my own flesh. Whole sections of my self-identity fell away like hunks of apical glacier.

"Go home," the voice told me.

"Sure, I will. It's not that I can't, or don't want to."

"You're not like me," he said. "You're confused."

"Are you hurt?"

"Piss off."

"Look, if you need a place to stay you can come home with me. You can stay as long as you want."

"Go piss on yourself, I said."

"Hey. I'm not one of *them*. You're not going to shock me. I'm just trying to help."

"I don't need it. I like it here."

"I was just asking."

"I was just asking," he mocked me. "You some kind of lawyer, or city bureaucrat?"

"You can see me; do I look like some city bureaucrat?"

"Could be. I can't see your face, only your shape. If I could see your face I'd know."

"I think I may know you," I said.

"I doubt it."

"It's your voice. You sound like somebody."

"It's the booze."

"Maybe. No, I don't think so. You can see me. Let me see you."

"You think you're in some goddamn zoo?"

"It's important. Come on."

"I've got hepatitis, if that's your angle."

"I told you, I'm straight—"

"What did you mean, about seeing yourself in the windows?" he said.

"I was on the way here. Running around the block. I can't remember the last time I ran. I'm on my feet all day long, but I never run anymore, not like that. Running for the sake of running. It was strange, seeing my reflection in the shop windows. It took me back. It made me think. My lungs burned. It felt good. It reminded me of things I'd forgotten, and some things I still can't remember."

"Bad marriage, eh?"

"Mm? No. I can't explain it. I've just forgotten what it used to be like, to look at yourself when you're young and strong and at least ambivalent about your reflection. Ambivalence, at times, is beyond my wildest dreams." There was a period of silence. "Did you hear me?" I said.

"I heard you."

"Well?"

"Well, what?"

"Is that why you're here, because you can't look into windows anymore?"

"You're not here to discuss philosophy, are you?" he said; there was a slight rounding to his jagged voice.

Ballad of the Confessor

"Not at all."

"Everybody like you wants to talk philosophy, and it makes me want to puke."

"Not me. I'm simple."

He laughed. "Good for you."

"I am," I reassured him.

"I've stopped looking into window years ago," he said.

"Oh yeah?"

"I don't bother to look up from the ground."

"How come for you?"

"You're not old enough to understand."

"Give me a shot."

"No, I don't think so. You might understand, and you might not. You'll understand when you're sleeping in my place."

"Tell me, so maybe I won't have to sleep in your place; no offense."

"You can't offend me," he said.

"Is it because of a woman?" I asked him.

"Boy," he said, chiding me.

"No," I said. "That's stupid. It's not the women. The women might push you to other things, but they don't stop you from looking into windows."

"You're right," he said.

"*That* has nothing to do with anyone else. Still right?"

"Keep going."

"It's *you*, you can't look at. Nothing causes you to despise your own image, but you."

"You, you, *you*," he mocked me.

"What that could be, who knows? A thousand things."

"It only takes one thing. The rest attach themselves like barnacles. Without the one thing the barnacles would have nothing to hold."

"I can look at my reflection," I told him, "but it takes some maneuvering."

"And a little bit of denial?"

"I suppose so."

"What is it, brother?" he said. "Tell me what it is."

"I'm ashamed of myself," I said.

"Of course you are."

"You don't understand. What I'm saying is, I have no respect for myself *because* I'm ashamed of who I am."

"And you think you shouldn't be?"

"No one should be ashamed of being who they are."

"Ahhh. . ."

I held up my hands in the light that came down in phantasmal shapes through the leaves. "These are the objects of my betrayal. They feed me, protect me, bring joy to my wife when I slow them down. Yet, I'm ashamed of them. I expect them to carry the weight of the world, and then despise them for their failure. I'm a coward, you see?"

"And your hands, what do they do?"

"They move things. Trees, dirt, manure. They rake, dig, pile, and unload. Menial utensils elicit menial expectations, from others and from yourself."

"Is that all?"

"That's all. You see, then, why I'm ashamed, and why I am a coward for it."

"You want something better, something easier. Something that will give you more money, and esteem in the eyes of others."

"It follows me wherever I turn; I can't help it."

"Would you like me to relieve you of them?"

"My hands?"

"I have a knife. I wasn't lying."

21

"No," I said, confused and startled by the offer.

"It's sharp. I sharpen it every day. I use it to slice apples."

"You're joking."

"I don't joke. I can still laugh, but I don't joke."

"I want to be like the others."

"Who?"

"All the other movers. I want to accept my life. I want to *enjoy* it."

"I can't help you there; though I've found if you accept your hopelessness, it becomes more bearable."

"But I still hope. I do."

"You've got a ways to go then."

"I have to."

"It may seem that way now."

"It's all I have."

"It's what's keeping you down," he said.

"What's your deal? Why are you here hiding in the bushes?"

"I told you, you're too young."

"Maybe a woman *is* what keeps you here. This might not be the same thing as not being able to look into windows."

He was silent. There was the strike of a match, and the shielded flicker of the flame. Then all was dark again.

"You ever hear of a place called Vietnam, boy?"

"Is that what this is about?"

"You know, boy, I don't know what this is about. Everything after my tour has been noise. I can't say what's what. I went in a boy, a lot younger than you, and I came out not knowing what's what. I like it here," Carl said. "It's home. I expect to hear the screams any minute. If I stay here, hidden, maybe they won't see me. That's what I used to think. I'd tell myself I'd stay hidden the next morning when they all moved on. I'd stay right in the same place until the end of the war. I wouldn't have to eat. I'd dig myself a hole and shit in it right there. Nobody would find me. Nobody would find me if I just didn't move. But in the morning I'd wake up and hear the others breaking camp. The darkness would be gone. I saw how vulnerable I was in daylight. I got so scared; you don't know how scared I was. You think crazy things when the Gooks are coming to get you. You think all kinds of thoughts when you've been where I've been. I suppose you think I'm pretty strange, sleeping out here in the park? Well, it doesn't seem strange to me at all. There's the difference between us. I don't see what you see. We're two space travelers momentarily joined in the same coordinates; but we're living in two totally different dimensions."

"I'm sorry," I said.

"Oh yeah? Why thank you, boy. I haven't heard that in some time. I imagine you are."

"Look, I have to go," I said. I crawled backward and stood up. I pushed my way between the building and cutting forks of the undergrowth, emerging in a burst onto the brick side path. I shook my head and brushed off, and looked back into the indecipherable darkness. "Hey," I called to him.

"What is it?"

"Are you hiding, or waiting?"

"You know," he said, "I really don't remember."

"I'm taking off."

"It's been a real treat."

"Sure you don't need anything?"

"Nothing in this world," Carl said.

"Okay. Well, see you around." As I turned to leave I reached into my pocket for the gum, and when I hooked it out with my finger it fell to the ground. I leaned over to pick it up, and that's when I saw his eye, caught in a wild rhombus of light, fixed on me. It was then that I recognized the voice and remembered him and knew who it

Ballad of the Confessor

was. I felt the eye on me as I walked down the cement walkway and out onto the street.

BALLAD OF THE MILLIONS UNHEARD

We go to the shores of the Cooper River, the hands of the earth. We go to the shores of the Cooper River, the feet of restlessness and stagnation and dreams. We go to the shores of the Cooper River, the backs of pharaoh, CEO, elected kings. We go, two-by-two, or in single file from shacks with bars on windows, pistols in nightstands, plots of kale and collards and squash and beans reaching to God's almighty mercy asking humbly, meekly for answers to our questions. We are black, white, all shades in between; men, women, children; husbands, wives, sons, daughters. Hand-in-hand we celebrate the bounty, or accept the harsh reality of the shrimper's empty net. Hand-in-hand we hope for sustenance, but will accept less. Hand-in-hand we have survived the flood, famine, and ravages of war. We sing the hymns of weariness. We sing His praise for guidance. The river flows endlessly past these shores. We are silent witnesses to the sameness of change. We watch, immerse our feet into the current pace. We come as thirsty lips in need of quenching.

The nets, I hear them drumming on the sand, on the docks, on the asphalt parking lot—there's a call: "Here they come! . . . They're coming! Oh, mercy!"

Ballad of the Confessor

There's more drumming of the nets, the readying, the nervousness and hope—the birth of song.

"Caught any?" the oldest man in a plaid shirt with bleach holes all through it calls out. He is the storyteller, the elder, the revered. There is no expression on his dark, tough cheek, except the permanent lines of witnessing and accepting.

"Not caught any," the one on the dock called back, stooped toward the incoming tide. "But I seen 'em!"

"Seen 'em? Aw, you only *seen* 'em," the old man said unimpressed in a toying, teasing elder-chatter.

The others clamor toward the water. Women, their pants rolled up, or wearing skirts that drop like crisp sails to their knees, or squeezed into spandex. Men wade in wearing faded, frayed cut-off jeans, shirtless, or shirts unbuttoned and blowing in the salt breeze, chests pushed out, always out, rugged, like battleships. Children stay back near the white buckets expectant, watching.

"Clomp, clomp, clomp. . ." then we cast. Nets are flung skyward, opening, seizing; they arc, they fall.

"Sssssssst! . . ." one-by-one they strike water, lead weights plummeting, dragging the nets in billowing cylinders of entrapment and conquest. Some count out loud; others count inwardly. The excitement tightens, constricts, chokes.

Arms pull. Baby carrying arms, tire rim straightening arms, asphalt spreading arms, weed pulling arms, sink unclogging arms, lawn mowing arms, harmonica playing arms, midnight drunken dancing arms. Arms, they pull. Hand-over-hand, the ropes come back, the nets unseen beneath swirls of green-gray turbulence close, collapse, entrap.

"Got some!" a voice skims from around the reeds, where latecomers and those who prefer isolation wade up to their chests among snakes and who knows what else.

"Me too!" hollers a woman, her legs like pillars tossing the water aside as she lumbers from the sea marsh, carrying the collapsed net in massive arms and massive fingers. "Three, four, five. . . eleven!"

Arms pulling, pulling. . . pulling, pulling. Nets held above white buckets—they are turned out, the shrimp fall with their antennae scissored and tails flapping; the sloppy splash of bounty, and sacrifice.

The shore throbs with hot preparation— *"Clomp, clomp, clomp. . ."* then the flinging, opening, arcing toward the perfect circle— *"Whhhhirrrrrr. . ."* and the net circles as they connect with the evening tide, exhale and now breath, twice each day— *"Sssssssst! . . ."* and then the pause, counting, imagining, expectancy; then it's arm-over-arm. . . arm-over-arm. . . arm-over-arm— *"Quaaaash! . . ."* the nets gush from the water, dripping.

"Hey, der! It's a good night," a voice calls to all who will hear.

"Whooooweee!" cries another.

"Hey, ho—the wind is calm and true."

"Lordy! Thank-ye, thank-ye!"

"Glory be! God, they be plentiful tonight. . ."

"Gimmee another beer there, will ya."

"Ain't that moon purty."

"That marsh, ain't she like a woman I knew. . ."

"No woman purty as that."

"Gleaming like new teeth."

"Soft like a whisper."

"All calm and orange. Lilacs too! Look at dem birds floatin' der."

"Full bucket already! Lord, they be plentiful!"

"Keep away from my spot! Back off, you!"

"But that ain't yours only, woman."

"Back off, you!"

"Can't we share an' share alike?"

Ballad of the Confessor

"Before I take a bite outta you!"

"Aahh!-aahh!-aahh!"

"Oh, Cooper River Bridge; ain't you happy tonight."

"Like a Christmas tree. Ain't we the luckiest."

"God, the picture she paints, dem lights a twinklin'. Cars look like little bugs—der dey go!"

"Oh, Lordy, it's hot!"

"The humidity!"

"Like tar."

"Honey."

"*Love!*"

"Gum!—Aahh!-aahh!-aahh!"

"Hey, girl. What you doin' sittin' idle; pop them heads off dem shrimp, befo' I smack you one."

"I don't *like* it; it's *mean*."

"Ask her if meanness don't feed her belly, Sammy."

"Beer! More beer!"

"Here, ol' Fannie; set your wide body down. You been workin' too hard."

"It's my hip. Sciatica. Arthritis is eatin' me up."

"You set an' let us do it tonight, woman. Der you go."

"Bless you, Henry. Some say you're low mean."

"I can be. I can be, woman."

"Tyrone; look at Sheila over there!"

"Sheila? . . . Little She'?"

"The very one. All grown up like a rose blossom."

"Sheila, in that short red dress; don't she know you don't go shrimpin' in that?"

"She knows. Oh, she knows it. But, she ain't here for the shrimpin'. She's here for the mannin'!"

"Aahh!-aahh!-aahh!"

"Quit, you two. Keep your eyes to the task. And *you*, husband of mine, you keep your eyes on *my* ass, or your ass is mine."

"Ass enough for three, honey bee. Jus' wait 'til we get home and—"

"Billy's got an eel! Billy's got an eel!"

"I had a crab, but I let 'em go—"

"Kick it!"

"Don't touch it!"

"Eeeeeeeeeee!"

"Ploppity-plop; bye-bye. . ."

"God must be a painter. . . that sunset. . ."

"It's Michelangelo doin' it."

"It's the Lord. Only the Lord."

"Michelangelo maybe too."

"Calhoun! Toss me a joint!"

"You won't drop it?"

"I won't drop it. Fire it over!"

"Here goes!"

"You two; shouldn't oughtta be smokin' dat. The devil's tobacco."

"Tired is what I am, Lord. Beat up tired."

"You've lived a good life, woman."

"I tried."

"Heaven's gate is wide open! Enjoy the moon! The settin' sun! Sheila's red dress! The smell of your brother's sweat, an' your sister's sweet song. The heat and stench and abuse and shame. Heaven's gate is wide open!"

We, the rodents dripping wet scurrying below the Cooper River Bridge, miles away from everywhere; we, hand-in-hand in terrible pain, swollen feet, knowing weariness and weariness' minimum wage replacement; we, the muted throng banging on the fence. Oh, the

Ballad of the Confessor

helpless, hopeless punch drunkenness of a silent majority, utensils still before science relegates us to the trash heap. Glorious is this life we lead!

WORKINGMAN'S SANITY

Yesterday it rained steady. Even wearing a poncho you get sticky wet. Your jeans shrink up and squeeze around your always-moving legs and add to the heaviness already there. Your socks become saturated. Puddles form in your boots. The heat stays locked around you, making it feel like you're stuck in a hot shower with no door.

Mike was standing beneath the trailer awning talking to Roxy. He's part of the landscaping crew. Bowman's the boss. There's Eddie, Mitch, and Mike. Eddie does about half the work while Bowman, who's this cranky old guy about Reggie's age, watches and directs and tries to get Mitch and Mike to do the other half. Mike says he's got a degree from some school out West. He won't say what school. He's a nosy bastard, but won't give up anything about himself. Mike's a bullshitter. Bullshitters, if they know they're bullshitters, only lose their privilege of esteem. But if you're a bullshitter and you can't see it when you look into the mirror, you better watch yourself. So Mike shouldn't have been surprised when somebody put a dead copperhead in his lunch box, or when they stuck an orange onto his exhaust. He shouldn't be surprised that Eddie and Mitch never ask him if he wants anything when they run across the highway

Ballad of the Confessor

to the Kwik Mart for sandwiches. He should know. But Mike's just an example for us all, and our selective blindness.

I don't know why, but I like him. I'm the only one. Everybody else hates him. Hate's a strong word, but they do. They'd like to see him in the obituaries. Roxy's the secretary slash register girl. She sits outside trailer A under the awning and rings up customers. She hates Mike because he's a touchy-feely sort of guy. The fact that he's Mexican—or Cuban, or Puerto Rican, or whatever he is—doesn't help. When somebody asked Mike where he moved from, he waved his arms like he does and said something vague. "New Mexico, yeah, out there, you know, like that," were his exact words. You'd have thought he was just asked if he'd ever contracted the clap. He hides who he is. Nobody likes a guy who's so secretive, but when you're a bullshitter, a groper, and a foreigner to boot; well, you're on everybody's shit list. I'm surprised he hasn't been lynched, really.

Me and Reggie went to the back of trailer B, the tool shed trailer, to get a drink. We'd been moving the new mums and bales of peat moss all morning. The boss wanted the new mums over where all the other mums were, and the peat moss stacked where the new mums were. We had the small tractor and flatbed trailer to make it easier on us. You can't always maneuver the tractor in the aisles, and then you have to use the big pushcarts. We already had the mums moved. We were halfway through the peat moss. Reggie drank two paper cups of water standing in front of the big orange water jug, then took a third and sat on the edge of the back of the trailer on a hammer and some extension cords. I drank three paper cups standing at the water jug, then took a fourth and sat down on a squashed box of drywall screws and some saw blades still in a bag.

"You seen the salt pills?" I asked Reggie. His small, slow-moving eyes showed that he'd heard me, but he didn't say anything. "You seen the salt pills?" I repeated.

His head came toward me slowly. His eyes floated between me and the side of the trailer. "Huh-uh," he said, and his body lurched like a hiccup.

"Who the hell's been taking them? If it's Mike. . ."

"Boss says he wants us to move some of them trees."

"What trees?"

"Big ones. I'll show you. I gotta receive a truck around 2:00." What Reggie was saying was, you're going to be moving them solo.

"How many?"

"Aw. . . twenty-five, thirty maybe."

"Big? How big?"

"Pretty big. I'll show you. You'll have to use the tractor. Take 'em two, maybe three at a time."

We watched as Lyle and Eddie walked past us toward trailer A. Lyle was a temp under Reggie. He was a huge, muscular ex-fullback for some southern tech school. Most recently he had been a Merchant Marine. They were talking loud, laughing, oblivious to the rain and mud.

"What's Lyle doing today?" I said. Lyle had been working for the nursery for two weeks, though you couldn't really call telling stories and walking from one end of the nursery to the other looking for your hat working. "Hey," I said. "Think Lyle can help me?"

Reggie's head came my way again; beneath the hood of his poncho his face looked surreally round and waxy with beads of sweat-rain clinging to it, then dribbling off. He was grinning. "Boss says he wants him to work on the woodpile." The woodpile was in the back of the nursery, next to the pond. It's where everything not immediately needed was tossed. Some of it was true junk, but most of it wasn't. It was like a teenager's closet, only on a mammoth scale. Lyle had been given the task of retrieving all the three and five-gallon plastic containers.

Ballad of the Confessor

"Is that so," I said, lifting my forehead at Reggie. We were both thinking of the copperheads back there around the pond. The woodpile was like a copperhead motel.

Mike came around and acted surprised to see us sitting there, but me and Reggie knew it was a phony surprise. My leg was in his way, but I left it there pretending I didn't know. Mike had to bend over and reach with his fingers for the water. He has long fingernails for a guy. His hands are feminine looking because they're so smooth with small knuckles and no hair anywhere on them. Mike had on a rain suit, not a poncho. He was some hotshot soccer referee. The rain suit was for officiating. It contributed to his air of superiority, and our sentiments of loathing. He spoke in rapid, expressive bytes of often unintelligible chatter. He used his hands a lot. Mike didn't know the difference between attentiveness, and glaring. Reggie was doing the latter.

He began to tell us about the proper way to fry a steak. "You know, get the pan hot." His hands were like a bunch of sparrows flapping around his soccer referee rain suit. "Hot, it reall—lly has to be hot, because if it isn't you won't get the proper searing of the meat—" his feminine fingers in an emphatic pinch— "It's the searing of the outside of the steak that holds in the juices, makes it reall—lly, reall—lly good. So. Uhm, first you put some butter in the pan. Real butter, not margarine or any of that other stuff—real butter. Let it sizzle. Spread it all around, but don't let it brown. As soon as it sizzles and is reall—lly hot, put in your steak. Maybe move it around with your fork just a leetle so the butter covers the bottom and it doesn't stick. Three minutes," he said, sticking up three fingers decisively like he'd just called somebody for a foul. "That's it—" and he cut the air with his hand now flattened like a knife. "No more than three minutes. Then you have to gently flip it over. Make sure there's enough butter still in the pan; you may have to add a leetle

34

more. Depending on the thickness, you cook this side two, three, or four minutes. Remove it and put it on a hot plate. People make the mistake of putting a steak on a cold plate. No good. It's got to be hot. A leetle salt, pepper to your taste. Serve it with some green beans, some rice or a baked potato." He kissed his pinched fingers and flung them our way. "Excellent! The proper way to cook a steak."

As soon as Mike was finished, without acknowledging that he'd heard one single word of his unsolicited dissertation, Reggie asked him, "You do somethin' with the salt pills?"

"Salt pills? What do you mean? Are you asking me if I took the salt pills? You mean the salt pills that were back *here*? What do you mean?"

"Mike, where do you live?" Reggie asked him directly.

"Where do I live?" Mike stammered.

"Yeah. How come you won't tell anybody where you live?"

"Where do I live? What's so important about where I live? It's just a place. You know. Like where you live. It's nothing special."

"Yeah, but where is it?"

"Out there," Mike said, flapping his hands in some nondescript direction.

"Out where? What street?"

"You know, some street. Nothing special. Just an ordinary street."

"I know it's an ordinary street," Reggie said. "You've told us that. Mike, what's the name of the street you live on?"

"What's the matter?" Mike became defensive. "Why does it matter?"

"It matters because you gotta know every little thing about *us*. But you won't even tell me what street you live on."

"Take it easy."

Ballad of the Confessor

"What are you, some kind of illegal alien? Why won't you tell us anything about yourself?" Reggie rolled from the back of the trailer onto his feet. He stood close to Mike. "Who the hell are you?"

I walked past Roxy, who lifted the pencil that seemed always in her hand and twirled it at me.

"How's it going?" I said.

"It's not," she answered. She looked the way she often looked: sad and bored. I stopped and turned toward her and we stared at one another. She, from the dry block of space beneath the awning, and me, from the pouring rain. Even from the distance I could see her open blouse, and the peeking bra from the slit made by the top buttons that were left open. At times half of Roxy's breasts, covered in a pink or blue Victoria's Secret bra, were on display. The boss' wife had talked to her about it more than once. The thing was, Roxy didn't seem to be a loose girl. She never flirted. She was like an adolescent girl who doesn't understand how provocative she's being. Or maybe she did. She must. How couldn't she? Everybody stared down her blouse. You couldn't help it, the same way you can't help looking at a man with a limp, or a seven-foot giant. When she wore skirts they were always short. She sat with her legs side-by-side so that her panties showed. She was the subject of conversation when workers congregated. Guys walked over so they could chat her up and look at her chest. Nobody said anything offensive, except Mike who liked to comment on her hair and its likeness to fine spun silk, or tell her how her skin was like alabaster.

"It gonna rain all day?" I asked her. She had a small radio that she kept beside her. On days like this it was all there was to keep her sane.

"I don't know," she said in that monotone voice and sad gaze. "I haven't heard anything."

She was seeing this forty-seven year old guy, some divorced

salesman. He had a daughter older than Roxy. The daughter, for obvious reasons, hated her. The guy was always traveling, never able to see her more than once a week for a good bang, I'm sure. A real prize. There had to be a daddy complex going on there which explained Roxy's side, but I never had the time or desire to give it much thought. The sight of her exposed breasts wrapped in pink Victoria's Secret silk caused my mind to go freewheeling as I got the tractor and began moving the trees. I wondered what they'd feel like against my cheek, or what they'd be like in my hands. I fantasized about meeting her in some darkened corner of the nursery and taking her, seeing those big white mama's jiggle, bounce, jolt. I imagined her whimpers, her lips around me. I imagined how like all women she became someone wholly different under the trance of lust. I wondered whether she shaved between her legs. I pictured her standing in the shower pulling up the skin there with one hand, shaving it, or trimming it. I wondered if she'd go for another woman, or more than one guy at a time, or a dog, or a horse, or a priest, or an uncle, or a Coke bottle; if she ever did it the other, unspeakable way, and if she did if she liked it, or simply needed to feel the taste of bearable pain that comes with recreational masochism. I pictured her face covered with come. Mine, and all the others; one after the other standing in line with her legs spread wide across a table in one of the greenhouses; her tongue, her eyes, her fingers, her hair, her willingness, her shame, her guilt. Once when I was looking for a sheet of plastic in the old shack back by the pond, I had to get rid of all the tension I'd built up thinking about her. I don't know how I'd face the world if somebody would have caught me. I got more work done after that, and didn't think of her again for the whole day.

When I was done moving the trees I helped Reggie unload the truck from Byrum. The guy from Byrum was running late. He said he had to get moving or he'd be in for it. Once I got there Reggie slowed down considerably and started gabbing with the Byrum guy, who was up in the truck sliding plants to me. Reggie hurt his shoulders a couple weeks back. He went to the doctor and the doctor said it was some rotator cuff problem. Reggie couldn't afford to take off more than a couple days, but when he got back a lot of his work got piled on guess who. All the heavy lifting used to be shared between us. Now it's all mine. Reggie's milking it, there's no doubt about it, but who am I to say anything? I can't afford to get fired. So my feet keep shuffling. My arms keep lifting, and pushing, and carrying. My back burns. Sometimes I feel it going numb like it's a guitar string and there's somebody plucking it not so nicely.

Today I was helping this woman load up her SUV. It was all white. The outside was all white. The inside was all white. White, white, white. She hinted around about how clean she liked to keep it, but oh if a little dirt gets on it, it won't be the end of the world; it *is* a four-wheel drive, you know. So, as I'm loading it up trying to decide if I had a blister on my toe, or if it was just a pain out of nowhere that you get sometimes and it worries you for a minute, then goes away forever, I tell myself, this woman has probably never lifted anything heavier than a gallon of milk in her whole life! My head started feeling funny. Things got swirly and dreamy like when you get the spins from drinking, and as I'm bending and lifting, bending and lifting, I'm watching this lady's handbag and it turns into a gallon of milk, and then into a plucked turkey, then a head without a body, then a big ball of iron; then it got colors to it—swirly blues and whites and grays—and I realize it's the earth itself right there in her dainty little hand, but she's acting as if nothing's strange, or wrong, or crazy. Next thing you know I'm out of the fantasy standing there not moving staring at her round little Jell-O mold breasts. She's wearing this gauzy blouse and with the wind the way it was and the sticky heat, well, they looked friendly like my neighbor's dog. It's like

I'm hypnotized—I can't break out of it. Then I look up. She's looking right back at me, only she's not mad. She's got this cocky, teasy
little smirk like she knows, and I know; we both know it's the heat
and tiredness in me, and it's the heat and loneliness in her, and it's
okay, it's really okay for me to smother my wild ideas all over her.
She even reaches into her vehicle to get her purse for a tip, and
promptly gives me an eyeful of wiry, sun-fried spider vein legs and
upper-crust bony ass. You don't know how close I was to, well, I
think you can imagine. This was all before unloading Reggie's truck
for him, but after moving the trees.

So I'm shuffling, back and forth, back and forth, carrying bushes
by their leaves and branches in my whory mitts; my feet are aching
from being plastered to the dirt all day long, my insides are rubbery
and I feel like hurling, or gobbling up a whole chicken—I can't tell
which—and I have to take a dump to boot, only I don't have the
time, I have to suppress it and let it dry up into hard little marbles
that I'll have to push out of my poor dehydrated body by pulling up
on the bottom of the toilet seat like a maniac, maybe giving myself a
hemorrhoid or popping the veins in my eyes. I'm thinking of the
bony-assed Jell-O mold breasted lady. She's standing right there in
rubber pants, a hot tray of apple crisp in her arms like Aunt Bee on
speed, thrusting it under my nose. In my weariness I reach around
and take two heaping handfuls of bony apple ass and I mash my
dirty, sweaty self against her—her serpent tongue rides through my
mouth like a Ferrari and then speeds through my ear like a snake all
wet and wiggly, and I'm listening to some never-sung ditty of dirty
hyena howls resonating from her thin-lipped sun-blasted mug. Then,
I don't know how, but Roxy's milk white bahama mama's enter the
picture—they're vibrating in mid-air, coming right toward me like
the runaway nose of a taxiing plane, and then I'm smothered in some
sweet smell I can't put a finger on; some food, or drink, or moment

in time—it's all the same really—and all I want are Roxy's Guernsey cow squeeze-squeeze milk udders, and the fishnet Aunt Bee bony-assed booty skank to have her way with me. . . It's in the aftermath of this madness, hours later, that I found myself sprawled beneath the big oak tree outside the nursery gate. I was on my stomach in the hot grass, dead to anything that wanted me.

"It's hot, it's reall—lly, reall—lly hot."

I heard the voice. It was Mike. I wasn't sure how long he'd been sitting there. He might have been there before me for all I knew. His voice was heavenly, like the sound of the train I hear each night as I'm sleeping, or waking, or half-dreaming.

"You look tired," he said. "Yes, he must be asleep."

In truth, I was straddling that fence. On the collage that was my consciousness, Mike floated with a large cylinder of salt tablets strapped to his back, like a tank of gas.

"Don't worry," he said. "I'll let you know when she's here. Don't worry, my friend," he said in a soft, paternal voice, and I felt him gently tapping me on the heel of my boot. "I wish I could tell you about me. I wish I could be one of your gang. Some day I'll tell you. Some day, maybe." He began humming. The humming soared through me. I wanted to lie on my face listening to it for the rest of eternity.

RAINBOW COWBOYS

I had Saturday off. The catalytic converter on the car—the whole exhaust system really—was shot, and so I took it to this guy Reggie knew not far from where we live in Mt. Pleasant. This guy, Abe, was going to do it for half of what it would cost at a garage. Abe was missing the last part of his middle finger, which gave me reason to worry. He had downy black hair below his regular hairline in the back, like fur. I stood leaned against the car while Abe did a preliminary look underneath. Lonnie was due any minute. We were going to kill some time at the beach. Abe wasn't answering any of the questions I was asking him, so I moved over to the row of big rocks lining the drive. They were all painted white, like piles of snow. I watched a skink run from under a pile of boards to one of the junk cars sitting on Abe's lot. It had a red head. Reggie told me the ones with red heads were poisonous. I don't know if Reggie was yanking my chain, but it made me keep an eye on him.

Across the street a woman was putting out clothes on a line. Some kids were sitting on bikes—one of them was spinning his handlebars. A child who was barely old enough to walk stood in a puddle with a sagging diaper, crying, watching the boys on the bikes.

41

Ballad of the Confessor

Two big, gaunt dogs trotted through the neighborhood like they were on patrol. I waited until the dogs moved along, then got up and went over to a stream that was connected to the intercoastal a few blocks away. Along the stream was a nearly unbroken line of wavy docks, forming what amounted to a boardwalk. Tied to the docks were johnboats and other small fishing boats. There were crushed beer cans in all the boats. Beer cans floated in the water, trapped against shore beside the other floating pieces of trash. I scratched my head. It itched something awful. I watched the little mud crabs; there was a spray on the water from a school of minnows.

There came a young man carrying something in a blanket. He wasn't tall, but his arms were huge, his biceps like two croquet balls. The man got into a johnboat hurriedly, pushed away from the dock, then sped full throttle past me upstream. He didn't even look at me. I was standing not five feet away as he went by. I sat down and stared at the water. The water smelled rank. I'm so used to the rankness it doesn't bother me anymore. In fact, I like it. I like it better than any smell I know. I began thinking about what I was going to do with myself. I think about it a lot. The sun was on my back heating me up. I wondered what limitations in my soul relegated me to this. I wondered why it was so easy for others. So easy, it was like a big joke to them. It became harder, as the years went by, to imagine anything else. The phase that was all *this*, was becoming my life's history. Across the stream was a jumble of pine trees. They'd been knocked down by bulldozers and heaped into piles. New, weedy scrub bushes were growing back—all confusion and agony and red dirt. It was a completely hopeless sight. I put my head in my hands so I could still see and looked down at my boots. Where was I going to get the money for a new pair of boots? God. I heard the tacky sound of the mud crabs still eating mud. I lifted my head to watch them. God.

William Zink

I was approached by a short woman wearing an apron, who rubbed her hands as though she were wiping them with a towel. She stood nearby without saying anything. She just stared upstream. I asked her if she was baking something.

"Your apron," I said, nodding, after she made a squeaky sound to communicate that she didn't understand me. "You look like my mom used to look when she was baking. I thought maybe you were baking something."

"He go up the river," the woman said in barely intelligible Italio-English. She rubbed her hands with more force, as though there was something on them that wouldn't come off. "He always go up the river with his dog. That dog his only friend. The dog go with him for fifteen years. He never go up the river without dog. They go fishing. Hunting. Running—" she threw her hand out, "—up in the forest." She turned toward me, this small woman, her eyes rimmed with permanent dark rings of worry, or perhaps regret. "He and his father never get along. His father always say—" and here she spoke like the father, pointing a reprimanding finger, " 'You bad boy. I ashamed of you. Why you always get in trouble at school? Why you not get good grades like your sister? The other fathers tell me their boys good boys, get good grades, not get in trouble. I ashamed to be your father. I ashamed you are my son.' Ever since he little," the woman raised her shoulders, her eyes rattling around, "he say these things to the boy. So look, the boy not want nothing to do with him. He say his father nothing but a mean tyrant. Breaks his mother's heart," the woman said, placing both hands on her chest, looking as though she might cry momentarily. "Break my heart too. He turn out to be just like his father. Not want nothing to do with nobody. Only the dog his friend. And now, the dog dead. What he going to do? His only friend. I his friend, sure. But a man needs more than me, his grandmother. He needs a girl, but he too stubborn, too hard. No girl want

43

Ballad of the Confessor

a man like that. Girl wants a nice, and kind, and thoughtful man. He may never get girl. He become lonely old man. I see," she said knowingly, nodding. "I see what future of that boy is, and it not good. My heart just breaks." She began to tear up. "What he going to do? Eh? What he going to do?"

As the woman turned and walked a crooked, pitiful line back to her house, I thought about her heartache, and how her hopes were crushed. There was nothing she could do for the boy, and nothing I could do for her.

Lonnie showed up a few minutes later. Lonnie's a good guy. We worked together a couple years ago at the plastics factory. He still works there. He's married to Emanuella. They have a baby girl now. Emanuella doesn't like Lonnie's friends, especially me. We hardly see each other now that I'm not at the plastics factory.

I got on the back of Lonnie's bike and we took off. We couldn't move too fast because of all the traffic heading to the beaches. There were lots of convertibles with girls packed in like new toys, and since I had on a pair of riding goggles and Lonnie's spare helmet I stared at them like some bad ass and moved my head extra slow like I knew something they didn't; it got me more than a few looks. Traffic was backed up all the way from the light on Sullivan's Island to beyond the intercoastal drawbridge. We got up beyond the peak of the bridge when Lonnie says, "Fuck this, man. Hold on, pilgrim." He veered off onto the berm and we cruised past all the cars until we got close to the light and he turned onto a side street to avoid any potential police trouble. We cruised around the island a while. Lonnie would slow down whenever we came upon a group of girls heading to the beach, and I'd reach out and try to slap their asses. Then we'd take off fast because most of the time those girls didn't appreciate a slap on the ass; they'd be hollering and cussing and running after us in flip-flops and bouncing hats. I laughed so hard I nearly fell off the

44

bike. We tooled around the beach road and stopped a few times to smoke some weed. It was still early, maybe ten o'clock. The sun wasn't up beyond the neighborhood trees yet, and the dew on the sea grass glistened. I had to touch it to make sure it wasn't ice. I looked around. You could see the wispy, fanning clouds being pushed across the sky, and that in itself was enough to make you want to sit forever and watch, and think, and age, and accept. It made you think of people years ago, or people today living in Africa, or New Zealand, or the Yukon. It made you soar, and filled you with energy—like you were in some space vessel gliding effortlessly between the stars.

"Where to?" Lonnie turned his head and asked me above the choppy idle of the bike.

"You wanna do the Isle of Palms?"

"Isle of Palms," Lonnie said. "Oh, yeah, man. Let's go!"

We got back on the main road and headed for it. Lonnie passed slow-moving vehicles at 80 mph. The houses flashed by like picture postcards. We crossed over the inlet bridge and were then on the Isle with its new money and pastel houses and congestion. Lots of construction crews and piled lumber and trenches dug in the sand with pipes lying ready to be buried. Lonnie passed the main beach. We were headed for the far end of the island where all the new money androids have their beach houses. First we made a stop at the Brew-Thru and picked up a twelve-pack. The shade of the drive-thru and the echo of the throaty idle of the bike and the mixed smell of sourness and exhaust and the working girl who looked like she'd had a rough time of it last night; it was like a wave surge pushing me above the horizon—the moment was beautiful as hell. When we pulled out and back onto the main street, Lonnie leaned the bike low and took it wide, and then pushed it into high gear in a matter of seconds; he decelerated and made a quick turn off onto one of the side streets on the beach side with their gingerbread houses with putting green lawns and brick driveways and names on laser-burned signs like, "Pelican's Cove," "Sea Escape," or "McDougal's Retreat." I never could figure out why people give houses names. If I had a house around here I'd name it, "Go Away." Or maybe I'd call it, "People Suck." But then sometimes I think I'd call it, "My Dick is Bigger Than Yours." I asked Lonnie once what he'd call his beach mansion. He thought about it and then told me straight-faced, "The Burp 'N' Fart."

The beaches aren't all private up there in Pastelville, but nobody like us goes there. We parked the bike, put the beers in Lonnie's midget cooler, and were on our way. We cut between "Moonbeam" and "Whispering Wind." The owner of "Whispering Wind" hollered at us to get off his lawn.

"Get outta here! Hey! You!"

But by the time he waddled his flabby office ass over we were on the beach and had our spot picked out down beyond the blonde lifeguard, between the Brady Bunch and the Cleavers. Neither of us had real bathing suits on; we just had boxers underneath our jeans. We stripped down. Lonnie looked like a piece of white bread on end. I was just as white except the lower parts of my arms and my head, which were black-brown from work. We laid out our towels and sat down. I cracked a beer. The Cleavers were building a Fort Knox for the Beave, and the Bradys were playing catch with a Nerf football. When the first drop of beer flowed past my throat and settled in my warm, empty stomach, I was shaken from my foolishness of trying to think about anything, and spent the next half-hour staring and doing nothing, like every other animal on the planet. Lonnie went in for a dip. He sweats like he's got a fur coat on. I watched him soaking it all in. He went out past where the waves were breaking and lay on his back and floated downstream like a piece of wood. Then he'd wade back to where he started, swim out, and do it all again. People looked at him and knew he wasn't Craig from the office by his whiteness and tattoos and boxer shorts, which were easy to tell were underwear. Pretty soon I had to pee and so I went in. Lonnie came up and we body surfed. It was just what I needed: to be thrown around by the turbulence and have my body pummeled by the sand and have water shoot up my nose and have sand wedged in my ears and up the crack of my ass. We came out of the ocean dripping and heaving and gasping and laughing.

"How's everybody at home?" I asked him.

"Homey," he answered.

"How's Emanuella?"

"Peachy. I don't think she likes you. But you should come over some time."

"And little. . . what's her name?"

"Gretel."

"That's not her name."

"Gretel's doing great."

"No, what is her name?"

"Don't you remember?"

"No."

"Margaret."

"Oh yeah."

"How about you; how's the woman?"

"The same."

"Is that good or bad?"

"What do you think?" I said, laughing at myself and the pitiful life I had. "Been working a lot. Reggie's got a bum shoulder. I tell you what, it's going to be nice when he's back to normal." I watched the sea gulls flying in place. I watched the dark, wind-swept waves. I felt the spray of sand on my face.

Ballad of the Confessor

"Bum shoulder, eh?"

"It's all right," I said. "What can you do?"

"Yeah, sure, what can you do."

"I've been thinking of moving. Maybe see what it's like out West. Can't be any worse than around here."

"Where to?"

"Don't know exactly. Maybe Colorado. Maybe Oregon. Maybe California. Who knows?"

"Shit," Lonnie said. "I didn't know."

"Ever been out there?"

"I've been to Texas. My sister lives in Texas."

"You like it?"

"I don't know," he shrugged. "It was all right."

"I've never been past Illinois."

"You should join the Army if you want to see the world."

"That's okay," I said. "I can see it without the Army."

"Don't knock it. It was pretty good to me."

"I'm not you."

"No, but I'm just saying—it ain't all bad. They take care of you in the Army."

"I don't need a mama; I just want something else."

"Go to Brazil."

"Now how the hell am I going to get to Brazil?"

"Fly," he said simply.

"I can't speak Portuguese."

"Hell, you don't need to know Portuguese. Everybody knows English."

"Do they," I said.

"How about Australia? Big place, Australia. Bigger than the U.S. without Alaska. And there's hardly anybody there."

"I don't want to leave the country. I just want to go out West."

"You going to do the same kind of work when you get there?"

"Jesus, I hope not."

"What'll you do?"

"I don't know." I looked at him and shrugged. "I don't know."

"How's the little woman feel about it?"

I shrugged again. "Haven't told her yet."

"You're not leaving her, are you?"

"Oh, no. . . I mean, I don't plan on it."

"You know she ain't going to like it."

"I know."

"Go to Montana. Montana's big."

"Yeah, but are there jobs in Montana? I have to go where there's jobs."

"Be a cowboy," he said with a laugh, falling back to his towel and spilling some of his beer.

"Don't laugh. I might do it."

"I always wanted to be a cowboy," he said. He had his bottle of beer on his stomach. He was looking at the sky.

"I wouldn't mind being a cowboy," I told him. "I want to live in the mountains away from everybody. I want to grow my own food, have a horse, some chickens. The stars, Lonnie. They say the stars are something special. I wouldn't mind being what I am now, if I could have that. Out there, it doesn't matter. Just like it wouldn't matter on Mars, or some other planet. It's a whole different thing."

"You ever ride a horse?"

"Not yet."

"You have to know how to ride a horse to be a cowboy. Think of all the competition. All those little kids out there who grow up riding horses by the time they're walking. How you going to get past them?"

"I can learn. You can learn things, Lonnie."

49

Ballad of the Confessor

"It's not the easiest thing, riding a horse. And then there's the roping, and fixing fences, and knowing how to take care of your saddle. . . aw, you can do it. I'm just saying it might be a little rough at first."

"I don't mind roughing it for a while."

"Sure. You can take it."

"I don't have to be a cowboy, you know. Not at first. I can be a cook for a while until I learn everything. Or even clean out stables—hell, anybody can do that. I'd move up quick. I'm smart. I could even start out working at a gas station—anything. Even this. I know how to move things. I know about plants, and manure, and what makes good dirt. They might even look at me like an expert out there. It wouldn't be for long."

"Call me up before you go. We'll have a good old time before you go."

"Yeah," I said, thinking about it. "We'll get drunk without the women."

"You got that right."

"I won't care what happens when I get home. I won't care what she says. I'll be leaving the next morning, with or without her. She'll know better than to make any trouble."

I rolled onto my stomach. Precious fragments of earth-matter blew across the mat of sand; they caught sunlight in their crystalline facades and it made me think of snow, the snow I would see when I moved out West. It was some time later that I rolled onto my side and looked around and was cheered by the brightness. I thought of all the places I could go, and all the lives I could live. From behind my sunglasses I watched Mrs. Brady. She was helping her boy with a sandcastle. She looked bored and trapped. I caught her looking at me a few times when I was pretending to look straight ahead. It was envy. She wanted our freedom. She wanted to taste risk again. Her husband a few yards away noticed her looking. He was some scrawny chump lying on a Ralph Lauren towel; now and then he flipped through some John Grisham book, and squeezed the Nerf ball like a real he-man. The woman got no sympathy from me. I wanted to ask her why girls like her always attach themselves to wood-brain goons who have ambition written all over them, when ambition is the main ingredient to a dull life? But you see it all the time; hot chicks trapped in the cages of doctors, lawyers, bankers, and middle management monkeys. Life is just college on a bigger, more dangerous scale—it's fraternities and sororities all over again. Lonnie, who can talk to anybody, began talking to her. He gave her a taste of his beer. Mr. Brady didn't like that one bit. He squeezed the Nerf ball and banged it against his chest. The woman was making an open mockery of him. Lonnie and the Mrs. were having a time of it. You could see her eyes giving Lonnie the ol' bump 'n' grind, and Mr. Brady's eyes killing Lonnie. Their two-year-old boy would grow up to inherit a fortune, be some big-wig at a bank or insurance company, and double his assets when the next wave of corporate mergers swept across the planet; I'll probably be loading up his Range Rover some day. We ran out of beer, so I went and bought us another twelve-pack. The blonde lifeguard looked bored just like Mrs. Brady; she smiled when I left, and then smiled again when I came staggering back across the sand carrying the thinly concealed contraband of alcohol in a brown paper bag. She had great tits and smooth, hairless legs. The first thing I did when I got to our towels was offer Mrs. Brady a beer. She took it appreciatively, not so much as a glance to her axe-murderer husband. Lonnie clanged his beer against hers in a toast to sunny days and penicillin.

We left around three and cruised the beaches on Lonnie's bike. They were loaded with girls. I kept thinking about all the attention we'd be getting if Lonnie had a really sharp-looking bike, instead of his beat-up old Suzuki 500. Still, it made a lot of noise. Girls go for loud noise and risk; they end up marrying security and boredom. We parked the bike and went in Ray's for a beer. Ray's is the big-time beach bar with volleyball out back, and bands on the weekend. It was nice and breezy inside. The beers were pretty steep, but the chance to mingle with brown, sweating, practically naked women was worth it. We stood inside for a while just taking it all in.

"Jesus," I said to Lonnie. That's all I could think to say. "Jesus."

"Come on," he said. We went out onto the deck. It was packed with bodies. I kept getting bumped whenever people walked by. Girls didn't seem to mind that their tits and asses rubbed against you, and some made a point of exaggerating it. There was a volleyball game going on, but we couldn't see it from where we were. I was hungry, but running low on cash. I nursed my beer. I had enough money to buy one more, the cheapest kind they had on draft. Lonnie drifted away to watch the volleyball, and soon he was talking to some girls. I moved off to the side so I wouldn't be in the middle of traffic and watched it all, thinking about Colorado. I thought about Mrs. Brady and her husband. I thought about the blonde lifeguard, and the Italian woman. I thought about her grandson and his dog. I thought about horses running wild inside a corral, and buffalo in great herds on the open plains.

I stared into the throng of glistening bodies. I have only one life, but I want hundreds of them. I don't want to sample them, I want to live them. It tears me apart thinking that I have to choose. I want to be born over and over, knowing that I've lived before. It's not enough being who I am. The world is wrapped in the invisible lines of peoples' experiences, criss-crossing the globe like string. It's beautiful and terrifying to think about.

WHO ARE WE, REALLY?

I had a dream. The dream occurred one day when I was lying in the grass beneath the oak tree, waiting for my ride. I thought I was dead. I thought, *Death isn't so bad, if I really am dead. It's interesting. It's more interesting than life was.* But I wasn't dead. I realized I wasn't dead a while later. It didn't bother me. Nothing bothers me when I'm dreaming. When I woke I had only the residual mood, and a vague notion of place. I throbbed in and out of consciousness. The traffic behind me along the highway reverberated through me in a pleasant way. I felt it in my ears and in my toes. Someone walked over my body. I felt the shadow on my back through my work shirt, and then the slight movement of the ground. I heard the sound of a car door open, close, and then the car driving off. I had this feeling that God was all around me. Without being dead, He came to me. I wondered, *Why are You doing this now?* And then I said to Him, *You know that I don't believe in You too often.*

The day had begun with my own human failure shitting in my face. I was on the curb waiting for a taxi. I had to take a taxi because she went into work early. She's been going in early more often these days. Sometimes I'll have her drop me off an hour and a half before

Ballad of the Confessor

I start, and I'll sleep outside the fence until Ben comes; I was too tired today. The guy was late. He was more than twenty minutes late. I started to get panicky. I was going to lose my job. I was going to lose my job because some taxi driver was twenty minutes late. I rushed back into the apartment and called the dispatcher.

"Hey! Where the hell is he!" I shouted into the phone.

"Sir," the robotic voice on the other end said, "the driver should be there any—"

"Do you know your stupid fucking driver is going to cost me my job!"

"Sir, I said he'll be there—"

"You people—" but I cut myself off, holding the phone in front of me. My hand was shaking. I wanted to crush the phone. I heard a horn—I ran outside. The cab was where I had been waiting, beside the curb. I ran across the grass that I never run across because of all the geese shit in it, and when I pulled on the door I said, "Where the hell have you been? You're twenty minutes late!" I got in. The driver got out.

"Huh-uh, man," he said. "Not in my cab, you don't."

"Come *on*," I said to him. "Let's go!"

"Huh-uh, man," he said.

"Come *on*. Get moving!"

"No," he said. "You don't sit your ass in my cab and get off like that. Hm-mm." He came around to my side.

"Are you fucking crazy?"

"Not in my cab."

I got out of the cab.

"I've been waiting here for a half hour! You're twenty minutes late! You're supposed to be on time! I'm going to get fired—where the hell have you been? Can you just take me to my job like you're supposed to?"

The cabby went to shut my door, but I stepped in front of him. His eyes looked at me with rage. Our faces were close. Our bodies were ready for anything.

"Go ahead," I said. "Try it."

"Aw, man," he said. "Don't *even*."

"You think I'm afraid of you? You think that?"

"You don't want to do this," he said.

"You don't either," I said through my teeth. I could feel my eyes exploding.

"Get away from my cab."

"No."

"I'm telling you." He pointed a finger close to my face.

"You're twenty minutes late. So now you're going to take me to work."

"Listen, mother fucker," he said, pushing his face into mine. "You move away from my cab, or I'm going to break both your arms and both your legs." He poked me in the chest.

I hit him in the face. I was too close. There was no power behind it. He was unfazed. He came at me wild and powerful. He grabbed my head and twisted it in his arms. I pushed him over. We fell to the pavement. He hit the back of his head hard with me on top of him. I was above him, and though he was moving his fists against me, I was the one doing the damage. I hit him in the face with solid blows that made his jaw give way with a loose, wet sound. He jerked his head in an attempt to avoid the blows, but I bore down over him and then I had him about the neck, choking him. As I was choking him my insanity did not fade, but something else—unexpectedly like a page from a book—fell over the insanity and coexisted with it: looking into his pink, desperate face, in his silent plea for life, I felt the most profound love for him. I wanted to go back, to undo the last two minutes. I was killing him, but as I was doing it this new, unexpected urge desired to protect him from his life and the men in them like me. I felt I would sacrifice everything for his safety. No, more than that; I wanted him to be happy. I wanted him to enjoy each morning as he rose for another day. I wanted his children to admire him, and love him. Mostly I wanted his wife to admire and love him. I wanted his life to be worth living. I spoke to him with grimaces and gasps— why couldn't he understand that I wasn't the kind of man who did these things? Couldn't he see it? It was there, through my rage. *Look*, I wanted to say to him. *Who do you think I am?* I wanted to really tell him. I wanted to stop what I was doing, if only he would stop what he was doing. I wanted to embrace him, to share what I was thinking with him. He pushed his thumbs into my eyes. I couldn't release my hold on him. Then, I leaped off and fell to the grass. I covered my eyes. I felt to see if they were still there. I felt for blood. I opened them—my left eye was blurred. I heard him choking and spitting. I feared that I had been blinded. I looked over. He lay with his back to me clutching his throat, struggling to his knees, coughing. I crawled toward him, rolling part of the way on my stomach, like a snake. I touched him, apprehensively.

"Hey," I said. "Hey."

I thought he would pull away, but he didn't. He wasn't coughing up blood. I was relieved. My left eye still could not see, though I tried to focus on his slumped gray figure. I let go of him as he staggered away from me, got into his cab, and drove off. I sat in the grass panting, but not for long. I ran the three and a half miles to work along the highway in my work boots. As I ran I tried but could not ignore the honks and other more profane forms of derision coming from kids driving by on their way to school.

The day was unlike all others. Nobody noticed that I came in late. I'd been working on a frame the boss was going to use for a water plant display. It was in the back. I said the day was unlike others. It's true. Not the events of the day; they were like all the rest. But *I* was different. I went through the usual motions of physical labor without realizing what I was doing. I moved like an automated machine. I was afraid. Afraid that I'd hurt the cabby, but more afraid that he had told his people, and they would call the police. I was a criminal. Whether the crime was reported did not alter the fact that in a fit of compressed rage I had attacked a man. Throughout the day I imagined the events as they had not happened. I invented a fantasy. The fantasy was impossible to avoid—it soaked up some of my guilt and shame until like all fantasies it fell flat and I knew again what I had done, that I was now in a different category of men.

Jim, who was an engineer but because of the poor economy was working at the nursery, came walking down. Jim designed the water plant display I was building. The boss used him for anything that required intelligence. He was designing a new archway that was going to go near the entrance of the nursery. The boss loved Jim because he was paying him not much more than minimum wage and he was receiving real engineering services. Jim knew this was only temporary. Often I studied him and then made awkward attempts to duplicate his carefree laugh, or his slow, cat-like stroll. I felt like a fool doing it. I wanted to be Jim. I didn't want to be *like* him, I wanted to *be* him. I wanted his swagger, his happy smile. He was right there, only a few feet away. Yet, we existed together only at crossroads.

"Seen any snakes?" he asked me. Jim had a hoe sitting horizontally across his shoulders; his arms hung over each side like prints in a darkroom. Jim was the resident copperhead assassin.

"Not today," I told him.

"Ben says somebody saw some yesterday. Be careful."

I wasn't sure why he'd come down, but now that he was here he inspected my work. It wasn't a complicated thing to build. It was like putting Lincoln Logs together. Any half-brain could do it. I felt humiliated, in a way. I felt betrayed by the boss for vaulting Jim over me in the intelligence hierarchy. I stood shifting my weight while he looked things over. Jim had a long, stretched face like an almond. He was tanned, with blonde hair and a rough, sandy face. He talked in a slow, gentrified drawl.

"It's looking real good," he said. He put a foot on one of the logs and dropped the hoe in the dirt. He clasped the smooth round end with both hands and leaned on it with his chest; with one eye squinted shut he asked me if I was all right.

"What do you mean?" I said.

"You look scared or something." Jim leaned heavily on the handle.

We talked for a while, and then he strolled back up to the main part of the nursery, chopping at the ground as he went.

I was sitting on the assembled frame looking at my hands. *What was becoming of me?* I thought. *Where is this all going?* I tried to focus on the work, but I kept seeing the cab—first from my apartment landing, then as I ran across the lawn, and finally as I reached out to open the door. Each time I got to the point of seeing the cabby's face, I aborted my thoughts by looking away, or concentrating on something close by, like the tilted-over Coke machine, or errant tufts of pine straw sticking out like wild hair from beneath the shrubs. I began thinking of Colorado. I pictured the mountains with their snow, the open space, and the clean air. The thought that something like Colorado existed, truly, and was not itself a fabrication of my longing, made me believe in a hope, though I could not grasp the hope, or feel the shape of it. *Colorado. . .* I thought, over and over. I said it in my mind. It became ridiculous from saying it without pause, and I forgot what it meant or why I had begun such a diversion.

Reggie came down the path. I squinted at him because he had a curious look in his own small, white eyes. I'd been pounding one corner of the frame to square it up. I stood holding the sledge-hammer in my hand, panting, sweating. Neither the panting nor the sweating was profuse; it was the product of normal, easily sustainable labor.

"What gives?" I said.

"You about finished with that?" he said, pushing his own sweaty body against me, like a swaying tree.

"Oh, I'm getting there."

"You feel like unloading a truck?"

"What kind of truck?"

"You ain't gonna like it."

"Probably not."

"Got a semi from California coming in. They called a while back. Should be here in about ten minutes."

"What's in it?"

"Full, from floor to ceiling, front to back. Full as can be. The whole thing's ours." Reggie, who himself was acting punchy from fatigue, pushed on me again. "Well?" he said. "What do you think? Can you help? You don't have to. Boss says you can keep working on the pond if you want."

"Who's up there?"

"Chad. . . Lyle. . . and me."

A high school kid, a huge ox of a man lazier than a bear in a zoo, and Reggie with his bum shoulder; there was no way they were going to unload that truck. "I'll be up in a few minutes," I said.

"Sure would be a help," Reggie said; his hand reached up and massaged the point at the base of my neck.

"No problem."

"You gettin' any worms today?"

"No time," I said.

"You'll get some tomorrow, son."

Ballad of the Confessor

"Sure."

"Everything all right?"

Reggie, who once was a sinner but ain't no more; who run out on his wife for her bein' a nag; who once went through women like sodee pop; who had up 'til now carried thousands of tons with his shoulders, and back, and legs, and grit, and faith; a simple laborer like me going through life one plodding step at a time; he looked into my eyes and I looked into his, and if the universe could only have stopped its mad howl in the darkness of space and time; if it only could have exploded right then while there was *realness* frozen in my weary bones, a real bond between me and another walking, talking, prostrate human being. If only.

The truck arrived right on time. As Reggie motioned the driver back, we stood joking and exchanging Reggie's bum shoulder stories. Nobody wanted to look up at the truck. It was like standing in line waiting for a whipping.

Reggie and the driver, a fat, bald guy with red suspenders and long sideburns, came walking up together from the side of the truck, talking like old friends.

"You boys ready for some work?" Reggie said.

"How 'bout you, Reggie?" Lyle said, wiping his hands together. He was always wiping his hands together for no reason. "*You* ready for some work?"

I was too tired to react to Lyle's soft dig, but Chad, who had taken to Lyle, snickered and added something of his own. "Yeah, Reggie. How's the *bum shoulder*?"

The doors were opened. There before us stood plant material stacked just as Reggie said it would be: from floor to ceiling and front to back. We started right in. Reggie and the driver got up in the truck and lowered the stacked plants down to bed level. The three of us on the ground moved silently, like ants, lining the plants in tight formations. As space freed up Reggie and the driver had to walk farther to set the plants near the end of the bed where we could reach them.

"Chad," Reggie said. "You come up here for a while."

Chad was glad to do it. The inside of the truck was refrigerated, you were out of the sun, and even though the distance from plant material to the end of the truck was constantly increasing, it wasn't nearly as far as Lyle and I had to walk. Lyle, who had only one speed, was humming something, and talking to himself. After two hours the truck wasn't even halfway unloaded. The deeper they moved into the truck, the longer it took to move the plants.

"Lyle," Reggie said with a swing of his arm. "You come up for a while."

When Lyle pulled himself up into the truck bed, the driver quit working and stood jabbering about this and that. I didn't pay any attention. I moved faster. My fingers ached from crimping the lips of the containers two or three in each hand; my arms hung stiff and low. Lyle hopped back down on the ground. I was thinking about Colorado again. *Colorado. . . Colorado. . . The first thing to do is get a horse,* I told myself. *You have to make up for lost time.* I imagined the horse. He came in all colors; his temperament changed from minute to minute. I pictured going for rides on mountain trails. There was a woman there with me in the illusion; not my wife—a hybrid of those I had known and those I dreamed about. She would be up on the horse, and I would walk beside them holding the reigns, leading us through groves of old forest and dappled light. She had long, wispy hair, exotic tiger eyes, and lips that hummed sweet melodies of secret sentiments. We stopped, I took her by the hand, laid her down gently like a new and fragile vase upon beds of ferns and moss, and I made love to her. *Colorado. . .* I imagined driving through small Western towns, heading out toward the phalanx of peaks that stood ready all around us. I imagined being freed from the invisible demarcations I had scored around my own being. My hair was different. My voice was different. We were lying in the back of my pickup looking at the stars. She rolled on top of me and began making love to me. The truck rocked, the springs creaked; the small utterances from her lips were softened by cascades of golden hair moving like sea waves about our faces, and her tenderness released from me locked plumes of brilliance and goodness and kindness.

We hit a patch of big trees weighing fifty to a hundred pounds each. My fantasy disappeared. I fought to preserve myself. I thought how those trees will end up in some new housing development hacked from field or forest; they'll have been moved by human self-preservation, but no one will know.

I fell unconscious again, and the dream continued. I felt the warm sun penetrating my work shirt; I felt the itch of the grass. I heard the interplay of moving traffic and a far-off barking dog. I felt unburdened being in His presence, and the secret sin I'd been keeping to myself all day through the cadence of sweat and strain was there before Him, as I suppose everything is. I saw before me an array of hands. Every pair of hands from every human being who ever lived was there before me. All I had to do was recognize my own hands, and I would be welcomed into heaven. Millions of handless souls stood waiting, and would be waiting for eternity, for they would never recognize their own hands. I rejoiced! The Lord smiled. My hands stood out from all the rest like a crying baby. I recognized them in an instant, and was led through those alabaster gates by singing angels.

BALLAD OF THE CONFESSOR

There's a man who comes this way. He passes not every day along the highway out front, but he is there many days. We see him passing only in one direction, south towards the city. Whether he crosses the great Cooper River Bridge and passes through downtown is anybody's guess. No one here has seen him anywhere but out there, beyond the chain-link fence. He may go beyond the city across the Ashley River and on towards Beaufort. No one knows. No one has approached the man. We see him, but he is not someone you want to watch for very long. He is a reminder, a mirror, a voice.

The last time I saw him I was working with Lyle. We were near the fence moving rose bushes. We were moving without speaking to one another, avoiding each other. It was after it happened. Before it happened we weren't avoiding each other. Lyle, who has a difficult time talking and working at the same time, was standing against the back of the trailer full of potted roses. I was moving. I get anxious when I'm not moving. I feel unseen eyes watching me. Lyle was telling me one of his Merchant Marine stories. He's a good storyteller. At times I'm drawn in completely, and slow, and nearly stop to listen, but then I catch myself and move again.

63

Ballad of the Confessor

"We was out near the Philippines," he said, rubbing his hands together in a delicate, languid fashion. Lyle has large almond eyes and sturdy facial bones. He followed me with those eyes, and gave the impression of someone who was just passing through, waiting for the next bus. "Man," he said. "So, when we get a day off we make the most of the precious opportunity. Near us was a Navy ship. She was sitting there I suppose waiting for orders. We had a good rapport with those Navy dudes. We would have these parties, you see. Sometimes on their boat, but mostly on our boat. We're talking bigtime, let your hair down, get pissy drunk social extravaganzas. Lots of poker, lots of money going back and forth. The party was on level two that day. Along with the Navy dudes came a few Navy bitches. They weren't supposed to be there, they had to sneak onboard. Let me tell you about Navy chicks. You want hot—not so much in terms of appearance or style—but in degree of raw horniness; Navy women can't be beat. Think about it. Away at sea for four, five, six months at a time without regular dick, and say she's ovulating too?" Lyle shook his head. "You got yourself a human volcano." He collected himself, then continued on with his big almond eyes blazing. "There was this special kind of poker game, if you know what I mean. These two Navy chicks, they wanted to play strip poker. No lie. Being the gentlemen that we were, we obliged. These chicks, I mean they were *trying* to lose. Before you know it, they're sitting on the bed in nothing but some non-regulation panties. Then, without the slightest bit of bashfulness, they're grabbing and poking some of us fellas who've lost all but the grins on our faces. These chicks were making it very clear, the choo-choo train was passing through town. We took turns at door watch, and gave those Navy bitches something to think about for the next six months. They must have each had twenty of us, and of course some of us went back for seconds." Lyle's eyes rolled back into his head and he smiled wide with full teeth. He rubbed his forearm absently, looking into the sky. "I got this one—Red, I called her. Snuck her back to my bunk after the orgy. She showed me some things, that girl did. She put these pearls up my behind. The Chinese women, they put a string of pearls up your behind, and then when they're ready to come, they tug on the pearls. Red must have learned it from some Chinese woman, or maybe a Chinaman. Lord. Suddenly, you're like a finale on the Fourth of July. That chick; I mean, she could not get *enough*." Lyle had picked up a potted rose. I thought he was going to start moving, but then he said something. He said something with a new voice, like someone moved in and took him over.

"What are you doing here?" he asked me.

"What am I doing where?" I said. I thought he was kidding around.

"You," he said, pushing the rose in the air toward me. "What's your game?"

"My game? I don't have any games. What are you talking about?"

"You don't belong here," he said. "You belong here about as much as, as, as that car over there. You don't belong here." He slowly came toward me. Suddenly, without warning, he was in my face. He towered over me. I dropped the pots in my hands and made them into fists. He looked possessed; I was sure he was going to tear me to pieces.

"What the hell?" I said. "Come on, Lyle—"

"You and your *work ethic*. You and your constant *moving*. You think I don't see it? You think I don't know? You think *they* don't know? You think your Reggie doesn't laugh at your sorry ass the minute you turn around? Reggie's bum shoulder. You should hear him. Your pal. Your buddy. Man, give it up, will you? When you gonna wake up and move along now? You don't belong here."

Lyle lifted his hand to my face. I pushed it off.

65

Ballad of the Confessor

"Back off, jack," I said.

He looked into my eyes with a crazed and lusty hunger. He grabbed my face in one of his huge hands—he had my whole jaw as though it were an egg he had to keep from crushing. His wild eyes were unreadable, but then his intent became clear. His lips like poison touched mine. I felt his body tense; his legs trembled. He pushed his weight against me as I fought to free myself. I thrashed beneath his grip and tried to scream for help, but his lips prevented me from it. I punched him in the side. It did nothing. He tried to push his tongue inside my mouth. I pinched him—taking a whole hand of flesh—twisting it hard. Instinctively, he turned back reaching for his side. I wrenched myself free.

"What the fuck," I said to him, still backing up, my arms like shotguns ready for another assault. "You fuck!"

Lyle stood holding his side.

"You God damn. . ."

"You God damn what?" Lyle said with an eerie calm.

"Who the hell do you think you are?"

He laughed, as though it had all been a joke. It hadn't been a joke. I knew what it had been. Something kept me from shouting out, or turning him in. The thing that kept me from doing it was a terrifying, but undeniable knowledge of who the man standing before me was: Lyle was my confessor. He was my confessor for my assault on the cabby, he was my confessor for a lifetime of buried, blurred acts of ugliness; acts arising from desperation or paranoia or a deficiency of some kind. My life has been a series of ugly moments strung like festering, rotten-meat-pearls around my sweaty nape, testifying to my waywardness and dereliction—my prodigal nature. I sometimes feel eyes on me, looking at each rotten gem with condemnation, looking up at me with suspicion and haughty self-righteousness. I see *their* strings of grotesqueness, often larger and more unseemly than mine.

Yet, away from the tug of our kind, for those who can hide behind polished mirrors and hidden passageways, the strings are invisible, the moments evaporate behind the cauterizing blessings of God, and State, and Corporation—it's as if they do not exist! But exist they do. We, here on the dirt of the earth cannot escape behind mirrors, or through passageways. We, here on the dirt of the earth see the strings of grotesqueness about our necks, about all necks. We seek no refuge in the law, for the law, standing as it does apart from justice, standing as it does outside the ring of truth, is often our enemy. Here, on the dirt of the earth, we confessors keep silent; it is our silence which confirms our guilt.

My teeth bore down on my tongue. My fist shook, ready, but frozen. I had the urge to kill the man standing before me. I wanted to kill him for many reasons. Most of all I wanted to kill him for reminding me of who I was, for pissing on my soul, for illuminating my utter helplessness.

Lyle took the tractor. I sent him off to get more roses. I sat on the ground digging an arc in the dirt with a stick. When he came back we didn't speak to one another, and would not speak again without the memory of what occurred that hot summer day, without my mind expounding on that single memory like all the hoards of tabloid newspapers, wanting to know what it meant.

The man came past us that afternoon. We were moving without talking or making eye contact, staying as far away from each other as we could. He appeared in the corner of my eye. I haven't told you what makes him different, outwardly, from us; what makes all who see him inside the fence stop and watch silently, and what same thing makes those outside who see him blare their horns in mockery: It's the cross he bears. He has it on a small wheel. Other than the wheel, there is nothing about the cross that is different from any other cross borne by any other persecuted soul. The weight upon the man's

Ballad of the Confessor

shoulders is real. He carries the cross along the highway for reasons only he knows.

SPHERES OF HUMANITY

Evelyn works alone back in the greenhouses. She plants seeds in flats, then later when the seedlings have grown big enough to transplant, she puts them into four or six-packs. When it's hot she works beneath the trees and then moves the flats ten at a time on a push-cart into the greenhouses. She arranges hanging baskets and clay pots, filling them with blooming annuals. Me and Reggie move these heavier loads for her. She follows you in and tells you where to put things. She's appreciative, and when you're finished she gives you the impression that you've just done something extraordinary for her.

In the greenhouse the light is soft and kind and gives skin an orange luminosity; we rolled whitewash onto the glass panes for summer, and it works like cheesecloth to make everything look better. Evelyn is old, but in the greenhouse it's easy to look at her and imagine a young woman of eighteen or twenty. As I move her baskets we chat, and I wonder who she was forty or fifty years ago. I wonder where she imagined she would be now, and if that 20-year-old would have envisioned herself poking holes in a flat of damp Perlite beneath two hundred year old oak trees, reflecting on a long and varied life. I think about the thing that burns in all humans, the

69

thing that some call a fire, but that I know is better left nameless. Evelyn gives me pieces of it, and from these pieces a picture of the nameless thing moves toward me through my mind. Time has taken it and not destroyed it, but buried it beneath the sediments of life's waterwheel, so that she can be candid, or even blunt, but cannot ever again be completely free with her expressions and, I presume, her thoughts. She is hiding too. I wonder what it is she hides from. It's easy to assume it's just age, and the looming specter of death; but there's more to it. With Evelyn, there is more, I am sure of it. She carries on invisibly beneath the trees with their songs of thick wind and thirst, and in the greenhouses, alone, perhaps lonely, as though she were the last human on earth, or the first. Evelyn seems to me a point behind a grid, pinching, drawing the life-grid toward her as though she were a center, or cause, or result. At times I feel as though the whole world is some musical movement at its crest, and some great tragedy or miracle is imminent; it all hinges on Evelyn who goes about her work like one who has taken a vow of silence, or who has been afflicted with some disease for which there is no cure or hope. Often, the intensity becomes too much, and I must escape it. I rush off, and then clutch myself thinking of Evelyn and what it is to be alone, once beautiful, now gaunt and frail and near death; but then I think perhaps she is standing at the porthole to something even bigger than an afterlife, something spawned only from acute loneliness—for Evelyn, solitary, unassuming Evelyn, could be the keeper of such secrets.

I was talking to Reggie the other day at lunch. We were sitting across from the trailers under the potted evergreens, keeping out of sight. We could see out to customers going by, and also to Roxy. From where we sat you could see her legs, and her left arm lying on the table, occasionally awakening to tap the desktop with a nervous pencil blur. If you leaned to the side a little, you could see all of her.

She looked like someone you would want to approach, because of the way the glare flattened her features and emphasized her general outline and youth. I noticed Reggie kept leaning to the side to look at her. All through lunch he'd lean to the side, stare at her, maybe turn his head at an angle. I thought he was looking up her skirt.

"Hey, don't," I said to him.

"No," Reggie said. "It ain't that."

"What is it then?"

Reggie began to tell me. When he did I listened with a reluctance; this reluctance came from the fantastic nature of his story, and how it mirrored my own recent experience: He said that for several months now, whenever he looked at Roxy, he saw a circle around her. The circle was like shined brass, so bright he could barely look at her; he had to look to her right or left and concentrate while his eyes focused beyond her. I looked, but only saw Roxy, the way she always looked. Reggie went on: He said he'd been trying to avoid her, but she was like a funnel cloud pulling him in. He hadn't told anyone about it because he thought he was going crazy. The ring of shined brass had a familiarity to it, but at first he couldn't say what it was. Then he remembered something. He told me another story from years ago: Once, when he was living in Baltimore working as a DJ, he met a man. The man was about as old as Reggie is now. The man came into Reggie's club regularly; he never danced or tried to pick up women. The only alcohol he drank was a shot of rum every so often, but it was a rarity when he did that. He'd just sit near the dance floor watching all the people dance. Reggie said he thought the man was stoned the way he watched barely moving with a drugged, gleeful expression. One evening while Reggie was on break he went over to the man. He wanted to know what kind of stuff the guy was on, because it looked to Reggie like it was something awfully good. The man told Reggie that it had finally happened. "What finally happened?" Reggie asked him. The man told Reggie everyone had turned into spheres. "Spheres like you ain't never seen before," he said. Spheres that was like nothing you could imagine, and nothing he could explain. He was in a perpetual state of ecstasy surrounded by the spheres, watching them, especially when they danced. He said he knew something had happened to him, some fundamental change had occurred in his soul. It was the change within him that allowed him to see the spheres. He said that they were always there, but he had been ignorant of them. Reggie said he'd always thought the man had been on something, but he never knew what it was. Now he was seeing a circle around Roxy. A circle so bright he could not describe it, or even see it completely.

"I think I'm going crazy, boy," Reggie said to me. "Don't say nothin', now."

I haven't told anyone what Reggie told me. I can't. For the past month, when I see Evelyn, there has been a large square around her. The square is thick, like black magic marker. It moves when she moves, as though it were a frame and she were a picture. Do you know what I think? I think Reggie is right. I think he is going crazy, just like the man he met in Baltimore was crazy. Just like I'm going crazy. There's a common element between us. I don't know what it is yet, but I think it has to do with weariness. It does strange things to your mind, weariness does. Sometimes I want to know what it is. Mostly I don't. I try to avoid Evelyn, though when I'm feeling unusually strong I can look at her outlined by the thick black square, and the symphony is there all beautiful and sublime. When the feeling around her isn't tragic, it's like an ecstasy I can't describe, the way the man Reggie met said.

INVISIBLE ROPE THAT BINDS

Reggie didn't show up for work the other day. The boss just said he wouldn't be coming in, and that I was in charge. All day I wondered about him. He didn't miss work for anything. I knew something was wrong and spent the day thinking about it, which was a good thing because it helped the time pass by.

When he came in the next day he wasn't himself. I didn't want to seem too anxious, so I waited until after lunch to ask him what was wrong. He told me his son's friend had been shot. He was shot three times. Once in the hand, and twice in the stomach. All three at close range. His hand was going to be all right, but one of the bullets passed through his stomach, into his intestines ripping them up, and came out near his behind. It made a mess out of his behind. The boy had an emergency colostomy. He was in good spirits, everything considered. Reggie said he seemed glad just to be alive. I asked him how it happened. When I asked him, Reggie's face puckered, and he winced like somebody put something sour in his mouth.

"Drugs," he said.

"Was he selling?"

"Don't know if he was selling or not," Reggie said. "But the way they shot him up, I'd say he was dealing somehow."

He said the kid was walking along the street with his girlfriend when a car pulled alongside them. The kids in the car started shooting. They hit him, then stopped the car and dragged both of them inside. They drove around pushing guns into their bodies. They wanted to shoot them right there and be done with it, but the kid who owned the car said there was already enough blood in his car and made the kids in the back seat hold off until they found a suitable alley or field. As they were going around a corner, the kid opened the door and jumped out, pulling his girlfriend with him. The kids in the car took off.

"He's just a kid," Reggie said. "I don't understand. What everybody have to be shootin' each other for? Just kids. And for what? Drugs? For kicks? What the hell's going on, anyway?"

Reggie looked old as he stood against the stacks of peat moss shaking his head, staring into the dirt.

"What about your son?"

"Don't know. Don't know if he was involved. I asked him. He says he ain't. Says the kid was just friends with the wrong people." He looked up from the dirt. He looked like a child whose father had just hit him.

"Do you think your son will be all right?"

"Don't know," Reggie said lifting his shoulders. "You got guns in the hands of stupid kids. Who knows?"

Bowman needed another set of hands on a job in the city, so I went along. Eddie sat with Bowman in the cab. Me and Mitch and Mike sat in back between the balled up roots and trunks of three small trees. Turbulence threw dirt and wood chips into our eyes; you had to squint, or close your eyes. All the blowing crap kept the talking down. I opened my eyes when we were going over the Cooper River Bridge and looked out over the water to the small boats that were just glints and specks, and wondered what sort of lucky man could be out on a boat in the middle of the day during the week. Through my eye slits I looked over to Mike who was asleep with his head limp and his arms crossed. I looked to Mitch. He had sunglasses on, but I could see his eyes through them looking back at me, and they made me think of things. His eyes were like whispering Sirens behind the glasses. Suddenly, I had the urge to give Mike a shove with my foot. Nobody would question it. He was asleep. Who would wonder about some laborer who drifts off, and then falls out the back of a pickup? Who would really give a shit? I looked at Mike's flabby double chin stuck to the sweaty collar of his soccer officiating shirt. I stared at that flabby double chin and it made me sick. I wanted to be the one who made it disappear. I looked back at Mitch, but he wasn't looking at me anymore. He was looking out over the bridge to the islands. He was dreaming. We're all dreaming when we're not in motion. I began to dream too. By the time a new Beetle passed us, I was deep into a dream. I thought about learning to ride a bike in my backyard when I was five. I remember it clear as can be. The thought of that day carries me to sleep, and makes torturous hours at work or at home bearable. I remembered going round and round over the blacktop on my cousin's black bike with its thick tires. We had blacktop in our backyard because my dad didn't want to mess with grass. That's the kind of decision you make when you have a child every year and a half for fifteen years. In summer we had a swimming pool. Our backyard was the place to be for all the neighborhood kids. In winter we pushed snow into a square border and flooded it and had an ice skating rink. One day in summer a black man was sitting on the crumbly cement steps at the front of our lawn. The next-door neighbor kid told me I should tell him to get off. We schemed over it for a while, and then I ran up behind him and said, "Get off of our steps, nigger," and then ran back to the bushes around our house and hid like an animal. The next-door neighbor lady was standing in the empty lot on the corner crying. My mom and I went over and my mom asked her what was wrong. The woman said she had burned some trash and accidentally put the house key in with it, and now she had lost the key and her mother would kill her. It shook me, seeing a grown lady crying about a lost key. My mom and I helped her look through the ashes, but there was no key. The old woman who lived behind us used to toss rhubarb across the chain-link fence my dad put up to keep all of us in the yard. The rhubarb grew inches away from my small, greedy hands. My mom baked rhubarb pie, and made rhubarb sauce with it. I remember the excitement as the old woman bent at the waist with her sharp kitchen knife to cut the big stalks with their huge elephant ear leaves, and how she swung her hips to toss them over. I looked down at the back of my hands. I rubbed them. I noticed the veins which stood up like a railroad yard; I wondered why your heart keeps beating. You never hear of hearts just stopping for no reason, unless they're defective. What I mean is, they don't just stop, like they're tired of the monotony. Why is that? I wanted Bowman to keep driving. Thinking about learning to ride a bike lifts me up; thinking about how your heart could stop at any moment pulls me down.

The house was in the Battery. It was one of those you might stroll past some hot evening, dreaming you might live there some day, but that you know you'll never see the inside of unless you're a plumber, or a painter. Whenever I'm in the Battery, I get this illusion of security. The world seems orderly. I get the same feeling from watching certain movies, or game shows. A tree had fallen down in the yard, a giant live oak. The lady of the house told Bowman that it didn't fall down in any storm. The night it fell was as calm as could be. There was a big hole in the yard now where the tree had been. The massive trunk was still lying there like a carcass, stripped of its limbs. Bowman was mad. It was supposed to be gone. That meant we'd have to work around it. It also meant the trees we planted would probably get damaged when they came to finish off the trunk. "Can't those guys do anything right?" Bowman said as we piled out of the truck.

We had the three small trees in the bed of the truck, and one large live oak in the trailer. Mike and Mitch started pulling the smaller trees toward the end of the truck, acting like they were anxious to get to work, when really they were trying to avoid the bigger work of moving the oak tree. Me and Eddie began scooting the oak tree down the ramp of the trailer, then started pushing it toward the stick that marked where the tree was going. It barely moved even when we put our whole bodies into it; there was a gentle uphill slope between where we were and the stick.

"Mitch, Mike, get yourselves over there and help move that tree, now," Bowman said. "Hurry! If you ain't the laziest bodies I ever seen."

Mitch and Mike didn't do much in the way of pushing. They steadied the tree and made faces like they were really exerting themselves, and a better acting job I never have seen. Mike blabbered on telling us which way to push, and what the upcoming terrain was like. "Come on. Teamwork, boys. That's how you get things done. Keep it up. That's it."

"Why don't you shut your trap," Mitch finally said to him. He took the opportunity to remove his hand from one of the limbs. "You know? Why don't you just shut your damn trap?"

"Shut up? Me, shut up? Why should I shut up?"

"Because, you're always yacking on about something. Yack-yack-yack. All day long."

"You don't have to listen. I wasn't talking to you anyway."

"You're like an old woman. Always yacking and never doing a

damn thing."

"Me? Me, never doing a damn thing?" Mike took his hands off the tree. The two squared off facing each other, keeping me, Eddie, and the tree between them. "Yes, well, at least I'm not a thief."

"Who's a thief?"

"I'm not saying anybody's a thief; but I know I'm not one."

"You calling me a thief?"

"Why do you look so upset? No one said you were anything."

"Listen, you," Mitch said, pointing a finger at him.

"I listen, but don't hear anything but a woman's chatter."

"You're accusing me of being a thief; now you tell me what I stole."

"Nothing. You stole nothing," Mike said, cutting the air with his hands.

"No. Tell me."

"I said you stole nothing. Go on."

"Listen, you little whatever you are. You don't accuse somebody of something like that and get away with it. You hear me?"

"How about the turkey sandwich yesterday?" Mike said, his hands out to his sides like he was ready to draw pistols. "I ate half—exactly half," he emphasized making the cutting motion. "And when we got back to the nursery, it was gone. You know nothing of that, I assume."

"You think I ate your sandwich?"

"Who else?"

"How the hell would I know? Maybe *you* ate it."

"I ate half—exactly half. And when I came back, the other half was gone."

"Mikey," Mitch said in a sarcastic, baby voice, "how could I have eaten it; I was gone all day long with *you*?"

"I don't know. Thieves have ways. It's not up to me to explain your techniques."

With that, the chase was on. Mitch grabbed a bale of pine straw and went after him. Mike ran in a circle around the lawn taking Mitch over the trunk of the live oak and through two small alcoves of yews. Along the way he picked up a small branch and waved it at Mitch like a matador's cape, taunting him. Me and Eddie stopped to rest and watch. We wondered what Mitch was going to do with the pine straw.

"Thief! Thief! Thief!" Mike cried out in the desperation of one who is the quarry.

"Illegal alien! Illegal alien!" Mitch, the pursuer, returned with the most powerful verbal attack he could think of.

"Turkey snatcher!"

"Yack-yack-yacker!"

"You'll never catch me!"

"Remember the Alamo! Don't think we forgot!"

Mike, fully aware that Mitch's vision was impaired by the bulky bale of pine straw, led him over a low hedge. Mitch and the pine straw went tumbling. Mike, like a hunter who's wounded his prey, kept his distance, waving the branch. "I didn't do it. I didn't do it. You did it yourself, Mitch. Don't get mad at *me*." Mitch left the sprawled pine straw behind, and took off after Mike again. Me and Eddie followed them. As we were running beside the house something caught my eye, and I stopped. I stood just tall enough to see over the bottom of a small bay window. A nurse brandishing a whip and a man in his underwear were jumping on a trampoline. The nurse flicked the whip at the man's behind, playfully, but the man reacted as though he had really been hurt and screamed each time the whip touched his pearly white skin. I watched them, thinking I wanted to jump on the trampoline too, when I heard a loud splash. I ran around to the back and saw Mike doing a dog paddle across a swimming pool. Eddie was on the ground holding Mitch by the legs, who was attempting to crawl into the pool; a Vietnamese pig was galloping terrified in between various topiaries and statues, and a topless teenage girl and a skinny teenage boy with shaving cream covering both hands like big dollops of whipped cream fought for control of a hose which had a nozzle like a duck's bill—the girl squealing as loud as the pig—trying to spray the foreign interlopers out of their small, private domain.

On the way home, Mitch rode up front with Bowman and Eddie. Me and Mike sat on opposite sides of the empty truck bed squinting at and past each other. I could hear Bowman giving it to Mitch, telling him to leave people's sandwiches alone. Mitch didn't deny eating it to Bowman, which meant he had done it. Mike, squinting, said nothing. I stared off past him at a gas station while we were stopped at a light, and then stared at the people who moved like reptiles, filling their cars. My brother entered my mind. There he was, sitting beside me in the back yard in a pile of leaves. Then, we were running together. He disappeared, and I was alone. I was cruel to my brother. He was not cruel to me. My cruelty came from my need for attention; his weakness provided me with an outlet for my loneliness. He became cold as he grew, and often I wondered if I was the reason for it, or was only the catalyst. My mind shifted between thinking of my brother sitting beside him in the leaves or running beside the house as fast as we could, and the reptiles at the gas station. I looked over to Mike, who was sleeping with his head lolling on his chest and his arms folded over his soccer shirt. I had an urge to hold his face in my hands and tell him everything, and make it all right. I never had the urge again, as long as I knew him.

THE ORANGE CHAIR

I pass the orchard every day. The orchard is vast, and kept tidy. When I pass the orchard it's as if I am looking at a twin brother, for it appears much the way the nursery appears from the highway. I imagine the laborers who work there. The tree trimmers, and sprayers, and mowers, and grafters, and especially in the fall the fruit pickers. Like the nursery, there is a chalky-gravel parking lot out front, and a small pole building behind it. Where the parking lot ends there is a small knoll. The knoll is covered with asphalt. The asphalt is gouged and unruly. On the asphalt is a telephone booth, and beside the telephone booth there is a plastic orange chair. The laborers at the orchard use the phone to call girlfriends or wives for rides. Sometimes I see one of the laborers really smile, and I wonder if he is listening to the sound of his baby's first words. There may be as many as a dozen men waiting in late afternoon on the asphalt to make a call. There is never a line. They stand in circles of two, three, or four, smoking, kicking the dirt, scanning the highway for girls, or slick cars, or some other diversion. During that time in the late afternoon the patch of asphalt is alive—it is more alive than any place on earth. It's the center of the world. Haven't you figured it out? There are thousands upon thousands of centers of the world—all containing epic stories that emanate out like spokes from a wheel. In the morning the chair and the telephone booth fade into the groggy mist of dawn, and often I don't notice them. They are there all day and night, the orange chair and telephone booth. To not see them is to not understand life.

It was a cold night when I went to see Carl for a second time. It was after a few hours of fishing past the islands up the Cooper River. Me and Reggie and Mike went after work. We caught some smallmouths, and on the way back Mike latched onto something big, but he couldn't bring it in. We had a good time watching him fight it with the cold spray from the bow flicking on our faces, and the easy bob of the boat rising and falling against the choppy waves of the bay. All three of us wanted to see what was on the end of that line. Reggie had to get home, so me and Mike went without him to Shem Creek. The bars weren't too crowded yet; just fishermen like us, and some other habitual drinkers. We sat on one of the back decks with our feet up on the railing looking down on the creek watching the boats come slowly in. Watching them made me think of this recurring fantasy I have of buying a boat and mooring it over between Sullivan's Island and the Isle of Palms. I've heard of guys who live on boats over there. Once you got used to the constant rolling, that would be some kind of life.

"You see my pole?" Mike said. His eyes were like black roaches, and I looked back at him hard to make sure they were open. He held a beer like the Eiffel Tower on his stomach. I never saw him look so happy.

"Wonder what it was," I said.

"Maybe a shark. You know, it may have been a *shark.*"

"Maybe. But if it was a shark it was probably only a small sand shark. Anything with real teeth would've cut through your line like *that*," I said snapping my fingers. "You didn't have a steel leader on. It could have been just about anything."

"Sure—how will we ever know?"

"Mike."

"Yes?"

"Could have been a dolphin."

"Yes. True. It might have been a dolphin."

"Do you wish it was a shark, or do you wish it was a dolphin?"

"A shark," he said.

"Sharks got a bad rap."

"No, it's not that I despise the shark. I admire him; that is why I want to honor him by catching him."

"But you wouldn't want to meet up with one."

"What do you mean?"

"I mean, you might want to catch one, but you wouldn't want to meet him in his element; while you're swimming, say."

"No. I desire to conquer him, not have him conquer me."

"You ever bump into a shark before?"

"Never," Mike said taking a swig from the Eiffel Tower now with its label peeled back in wet a curl.

"Me neither. But I know people who have."

"Were they attacked?"

"I know two who've had run-ins. Neither one was attacked. It just made them fear the water."

"I have had no such run-ins; and so I am fearless of the water. I cannot say I am fearless of the shark. But my history with him is empty. I can look toward the sea and believe my small circle of existence to be immune to the unpredictable target of his hunger, or rage. I admit, it is irrational, and it is baseless. But, it is there and I will use it until I do have an encounter and live to tell about it. Then, I will have the fear like others. How such an encounter will affect me—I do not know."

I was watching a Boston Whaler puttering past. I wished I was down there, and someone else was up here envying me. The light from the bow and stern was twisted by the dark creek, and reached me like sensual music.

"Another beer?" Mike said, but before I could think about it he'd flagged the waitress down and ordered two more. Mike was good at things like flagging down waitresses. He had an authoritative ease that I reasoned had come from officiating soccer games.

"Mike."

"Stay," he said, and thinking I was going to leave lifted his hand as though to quiet a room. "Stay a leetle longer."

"Mike," I said, "where *do* you come from? I thought you might tell me. I won't say anything."

"You're curious? About *me*, you're curious?" None of his usual defensiveness was there in his voice. The waitress came out with our beers, and then left us, and we were alone again in the corner with the cool breeze and mercurial light of the creek.

"You don't have to."

"Do the others also wonder about me?"

"They do. They think you're here illegally, which none of them care about. The only thing they care about is somebody who hides things."

"And they have nothing to hide?"

"Maybe they do, maybe they don't. I think the fact that you're always asking questions and never giving answers is what gets them going. It's a bad combination."

"They think I am nosy?"

"You do ask a lot of questions."

Mike was quiet. We watched the creek. The deck was filling up with loud kids. I began to feel their eyes.

"I am running," Mike said to me. "Running. That is my secret."

I looked over at him; he declined to meet my gaze, but looked out over the railing to the water. I took a sip. "Running from what?"

"I am sorry. I cannot tell even you. The running is not over, and though I trust you more than anyone else, still, I have too much to lose by disclosing who my pursuers are, and why they are after me."

"You have a family?"

"A wife, and children." Mike's voice became contained in a frequency that was both delicate and courageous. "I have not seen them for two years now. It is all I can think about, and yet what I must not think about if I am ever to see them again."

"Is there anything I can do? I don't have much money," I said, "but maybe there's something."

"Nothing. There is nothing anyone can do."

"Are they killers?"

"They are the agents of a disease called homogeneity. I was seen as a bee floating in a bucket of milk. My existence threatens them. They search for me so they might decapitate one more voice against their own hymns of repression and institutionalized control. It is dangerous for me to speak of it. It is dangerous for my family."

"Can't our government help?"

Mike moved in his seat and went to say something, then looked away uneasily. "No, my friend. That is not a place I can turn to for a remedy."

Nothing more was said about it. The gentle breeze rising from the creek penetrated my shirt and made me shiver. I thought about what Mike had told me, but knew that I was impotent on many levels to react to it, and seldom did I ever cull it from my mind to regurgitate it; it was there like a foreign object implanted in my body, something I was vaguely aware of, but nothing that changed my behavior or even my attitude toward him. He was on his own, as

85

Ballad of the Confessor

Reggie was on his own dealing with his boy who at any minute might get shot, and Roxy was on her own lying prostate to something that rendered her like an open carton of eggs, and I was on my own trying to bust out of the whole thing. We can confess, we can commiserate, but we can't truly help one another.

"Mike," I said standing up. My legs were stiff and unsteady. "I'm moving on."

"You're leaving?"

"Afraid so."

"We shall talk again some other night—mm?"

"Mike," I said leaning over, and when I did I felt myself teetering. "If you stare at her tits long enough, they might just jump into your lap."

I left him. After I'd made my way through the crowd, I looked back. He waved. He looked about as happy as a man could be.

The Cooper River Bridge was all mine as I went over it. There were lights from fishing boats on the left, in the bay, and also on the right, at the mouth of the river and beyond. I saw small flickering glows along the shore and knew they were campfires. I wanted to be over there sitting around the fires, among strangers who together comprise the immeasurable majority known as the sufferers, derelicts, and beasts of human existence. I sometimes fear the bridge. At night it hums, the steel becomes animate, it invites you through a hole and then to a ledge. But then you reach the summit of the bridge and see the other side to the shipyards, and the city, and though the city may appear shabby or grim from that height, it's not what it is that pulls you toward it, but the relief it offers from what you are: It is not the keeper of my secrets, the weight of my sins, the fear lying on my bed pillow, or the silence which grabs me after a week of toiling. The city is my pole for walking on wires.

The sidewalk moved with Palmetto bugs, crossing my path like caramel shadows. The streets were hushed by the darkness, except near bars and restaurants. I wanted to enter them, but I was low on cash. Anyway, there was no point. I came upon a café where a few stragglers sat slumped around small wrought-iron tables. I watched this young couple. Both of them were sloppy drunk. The girl several times slipped down her seat and nearly fell to the ground before the boy pulled her back up. She laughed beneath a shield of hair as the boy rubbed his hand up along one of her legs to the hem of her short skirt, and with the other hand he seemed to be tickling her nose and ears. She leaned over and licked more than kissed him, then slumped back, her legs sprawled and hands, brown from sun, clutching the iron weave of the chair. Seeing her brown young hand made me think of things, and my heart moved ahead of me. I was hiding behind the downspout in the shadow observing them. I closed one eye and peered through the slit between the downspout and the wall. They got up, supporting each other like leaning poles, and were across the alley on the other side of the street when the girl remembered her purse. She ran back for it. The sound of her heels bounced off the facades of sleeping brick and stucco. It was maddening. She snatched her purse and when she turned back toward the alley her body twisted, then froze for only a fragment of time into fluid color, and there was a shout from some sudden gargantuan hammering down on my head. I fell to the ground cradling my skull—I feared it would explode or be crushed—and I watched the girl with her shimmying hips of color and flashing legs and purse whipping like a tail cozy up to her boyfriend, who collected her under an arm and reeled her in.

I walked to the end of the Battery and stood looking out to the harbor lights on the other side. The space behind me lay open—too open; the cannons, and trees, and wide swaths of grass nipped at me as though I were something needful and rare and valuable, but I knew not to believe such falsehoods and cut a line diagonally across the space into the zebra shadows of floating limbs and witch hair moss hanging limp in the chilled evening, past more wrought-iron, undulating sidewalks, and pastel mansions muted by the night.

"Carl," I said aloud to the tunnel of shadow through which I found myself walking at an ever-increasing pace. The pavement did not approach me fast enough. I wish I could say what drew me toward the park, but I don't know. To this moment, I don't know. I believed he would be there. I had envisioned him not too often, only randomly at night when I couldn't sleep, or in half-second mind bursts that bombard me daily as I am pushing or pulling, and mean nothing. Now, as I was nearing the entrance to the park, I thought of all the days that had passed since I first saw him. I pictured him lying beneath the bushes, alone. The image bore down on me in that instant and crushed me.

I entered through the main walkway. I heard rustling leaves above from the slow movement of the large, rainbow-colored birds that live in the treetops. I glanced up, but could see only the darkness of the trees interrupted by holes of purple night sky. I knew that he could see me coming. As I drew close to the back of the park I looked for him. The shadows were too complete. I could see nothing of him. I stopped where the sidewalk reaches its deepest point and begins to curve back around. I was cold. I blew into my hands to warm them.

"Hello?" I said. "Are you there?—it's me. The guy from before. Will you say something if you're there?"

I waited. I kept looking behind me. My eyes were alert.

"I don't know if you're there. Say something, if you are."

No sound came from beneath the bushes. I listened closely. There was nothing at all. I began to believe he wasn't there. I moved my head in unusual and difficult to hold angles, looking at the jagged edges of leaves, thinking that maybe he was right there very close. I decided to sit down. I sat with my legs crossed, my hands hanging from my knees. I was afraid. I am afraid often anymore. It enlarges, the fear, like a plume of smoke. I have weapons against the fear. When the weapons don't work, I become an outsider from my own self. I go into hiding and I am ruled by momentum, and from this momentum I crash through windows and produce holes in my self-built zeppelin in my attempt to sit where I sat before. I never find the same place. It's worrisome, the same way it's worrisome to think about your teeth slowly decaying, or the earth's orbit slowly deteriorating. I don't crumble when I find a different place, I just change the level of my expectations. I readjust them each day. Afterwards, for days or weeks, I live by them, and so am defined by their limits. I wanted to sob right then. I wanted to take a stick and ram it up both my ends. I wanted more alcohol, or a girl, or both. I wanted to hurt someone. I wanted to dominate those who dominate me now. I wanted another life, another home, another time, another planet, another face. I loathed who I was. I loathed myself more for not being able to change anything. But I have been tweaking the dials of my life since I can remember; hating myself, loving myself, wanting what I don't have, can't have, and never will have. When I was younger I believed there would come a day when it would all be over, life would be predictable and orderly, like the clock on my bookcase. I used to believe that. When I was younger I believed in themes, and purposes. I used to believe in designs. I am too beaten to believe any of that anymore. Maybe I will be further beaten, and from it a new belief will emerge from the pit of my soul. I still believe in something. I just don't know what it is.

"Why won't you talk to me?" I said to the bushes. "This isn't your private park, you know. You and your little knife."

My weariness combined with my drunkenness to render me slug-

Ballad of the Confessor

gish, and dejected. I began to think about the tree. I've told no one about it before. When I was ten, my mom was weeding and came across it amidst the pachysandra. Then, it was only a sapling. Not even that—it was just a stick. She told me to pull it out. I didn't want to, but I did. I used all my weight and leverage, and after some wiggling and digging it was unearthed and in my hand. My mom was pleased, but I felt very bad. I didn't know what to do with it. I stood beside her holding the stick-tree as she continued to weed; the love for her that I always felt when we were alone together in the garden, was broken by the act of pulling up the tree. I wanted to undo it, to put it back where it was. She would not let me do that, I knew. I asked her if I could plant the tree in the backyard. She said I could. Immediately, I put the tree in a bucket of water; I walked beneath the ancient, giant oaks trying to project both daily and seasonal sunshine, and where there would be the most room for a rising tree. I marked the spot by making a divot with my heel. My mom believed the tree would die. I know this now, but didn't know it then. The tree thrived. I watched it every day that first summer, watering it, looking for small positive signs like new leaves, or later in autumn, the formation of buds. In winter I would stand staring at the tree for long periods, usually at night, alone, allowing snow to pelt my face. As it grew, I selectively trimmed the lower branches, and it became an aesthetically pleasing tree. It grew straight, and vigorously. One day years later I came home to find my mom and dad in the backyard. They had lopped the tree in two. My dad was struggling to saw the stump down. He asked me to give him a hand. I cried out, "What are you doing? Why did you do that?" They said the tree was a nuisance. It produced too many leaves to rake in the fall. I said, "What the hell are you talking about?—there're giant oak trees all around—you think this little tree is going to make any difference in—" "—are you out of your mind?" I ran away. It sounds crazy, but I loved the tree more than anything at that time. I may have loved the tree more than anything I have ever loved. When they cut it down, I became a vagrant, and have been a vagrant looking over my shoulder, or anxious for what lies beyond a corner, or over a hill, ever since. The finality of a hopeless existence prods me toward religion; if I could only convince the witness seated at the gates of my soul. . . But, I was not thinking of that event. I was thinking of the tree as it was in life through the seasons, and the pleasure I got from just looking at it. I remembered its shape, and then imagined how it would have been if it had not been cut down. I still have the tree. Because my father couldn't sever the trunk, I went out after dark and with my hatchet finished it off. I took the trunk into my bedroom. I have kept it with me in my bedroom wherever I go. Some day I'll make a cane out of it, and it will go with me into my grave. We'll move together away from this terrestrial prank; I'll walk past the waiting, handless souls, those who know no real sweat, no real ache, no real fatigue. The gates will part. My brothers and sisters, those who've been abused, overworked, crushed—they'll greet me. There'll be nothing but beautiful, callused hands caressing me.

HEAVEN AND HELL

It rained all day the day the awning fell. It fell late in the afternoon, coming down in a crash you could hear all across the nursery. Roxy was unharmed. It seemed impossible when me and Reggie came running over—the awning was a crumpled death pile. Nobody knew how she emerged unhurt. Within a week a new, identical awning was erected by Jim. Everyone forgot about the old awning that fell; but we didn't forget about Roxy and her good luck.

Me and Reggie were in the side-by-side port-o-pots. The port-o-pots smell, but they're clean because if you were to mess one up everybody would know you did it, and you'd probably get lynched. It took me a month to get used to the smell, but now it's only a test of my tolerance and I look forward to it. It gives me a chance to overcome something each day. We cut a small hole in the inside walls so we can pass reading material back and forth. I like *National Geographic*, Reggie likes *People Magazine*. There's no light inside. You have to crack the plastic door open with your foot.

"Jesus," I said. "Look at the size of this beetle." I rolled up the *National Geographic* and passed it to him through the hole.

"Good Lord," Reggie said. "That's life size."

"Yeah, I know," I laughed all giddy-nervous.

"South America beetle, it says. We ain't got no beetles that size around here. Seen some big beetles, but Lordy. . ."

"Pretty, though."

The end of the rolled up magazine came back through the hole. I read about the beetle. After reading it, I looked down between my legs and on the walls, then pushed my foot farther into the door wedge so more light came in.

"You ever thought of going down the Amazon?" I said.

"What?"

"I said, have you ever thought of taking a trip down the Amazon?"

"The Amazon? Ain't that in South America?"

"Yeah," I said, then waited. "Well?"

"Naw," Reggie's muffled response came back. "Not after seeing what kind of beetles they got, I don't."

"I wanna see it," I said to him. "Before it's all cut down."

"You wanna come to church?"

"What?" I said.

"I said, you wanna come to church?"

"Your church?"

"My sister's church. You wanna come?"

"I'd like to. But, I ain't ready yet."

"Ready as I was."

"I don't know."

"Mike's been coming."

"I thought Mike was Catholic."

"He is Catholic."

"Then how's he going to your church?"

"He goes to both now. Mike's not so bad."

"Let me think about it."

"Okay. Think about it. If you don't go this week, I'll ask you again next week, same as I always do."

"I appreciate it, though."

"Hey."

"What?"

"It would be my honor for you to come to my sister's church some day."

"Thanks."

"You need anything?"

"Need anything? What do you mean?"

"Ever you need anything, you let me know. Everything all right at home?"

I waited. When I realized that he was waiting too I said, "No broken bones yet."

"Son," he said.

"There's nothing you can do."

"Maybe there is, maybe there isn't. It ain't none of my business, except for you being my friend."

"Reggie?"

"Yeah?"

"What can I do?"

"Pray, son."

"I do. I pray every step of every day. Nothing changes. It's getting worse."

"Can't let it get no worse," he said. "Maybe you need to get some professional help. Having good people around you helps."

"But, I can't tell anyone."

"People'll understand."

"No they won't."

"Let them hear the whole story. I understand. They'll understand."

"It won't come out the way it really is. Then, I'll be—" "—they'll think it was me."

"No, son."

"You know as well as me, Reggie, truth is your weakest defense. When they've already made up their minds, truth doesn't mean a thing."

"You know the truth. And I know the truth. Why you care what anybody else thinks?"

"Because, it would be too shameful. Wherever I went, people would talk."

"Stupid talk by stupid people. Why you care?"

"It might be stupid talk by stupid people, but others will hear it, and believe it. And some of it will be true. They'll bang on the truthful parts like a drum. I won't be able to explain things to them. Then there's the law to worry about."

"Why you worried about the law?"

"The same reason you're worried about the law."

"It ain't the same thing. You're white."

"But I'm a man. In domestic violence cases, that makes me black."

"You think they won't believe police reports? Show them your police reports."

I shook my head and kicked the plastic door. "Reggie, it just doesn't matter. There's no defense against a crying woman."

"You can't go on the way things are."

"Sure, I can. I always do."

"You wanna end up crazy? In jail maybe?"

"It's hard for me to think about it. It's like any other addiction."

"See? You said for yourself what it is."

"I know what it is. But that doesn't mean I can beat it."

"You just gotta leave, that's all."

Ballad of the Confessor

"I can't yet."

"How come you can't?"

"I just can't."

"You can."

"You don't understand. I'm just plain sick, Reggie."

"I wanna help you, son."

"I know you wanna help me; but I can't be helped yet."

"Open up, and let the good Lord in."

"The door's open all day long. He can come in any time He wants."

The smell began to get to me. I felt like I was in hell. I thought, hell is spending eternity in a shitter next to someone who wants to help you, and not being ready to accept it. I had to get out, but the rain coming in soothing bursts on the roof of the port-o-pot held me back. Not because I didn't want to step out into it, but because it lulled me into a strange mood of perverseness; it made me think more about hell, but then about heaven. I wondered what heaven was really like. It must be some sort of perpetual ecstasy, combined with poor memory so you won't get accustomed to it, and then bored. Maybe like the first time you took a car out on a country road after getting your license, over and over, day after day, each time as fresh as the first. Or drinking beer after work each night and never getting a hangover in the morning, or getting fat. Or sitting on the back stoop of the apartment watching the chimney swifts, and later on bats, before going to bed. I always run into problems thinking about heaven. I can't interpolate between animate and spiritual joy— the human demands of work, of physical labor, crowd into my fantasies and soon I begin thinking about heaven in terms of the only things I know, like having a really good pair of new boots that don't need breaking in, or the climate changing so it's like Oregon everywhere, all cool and misty, or having my own car that doesn't need

William Zink

fixing; it's reduced to trivialities, and I'm left feeling depressed and hopeless. I can't figure out how I'll break out of this working class mentality. Sometimes it gets so dark I can't see, and I open my eyes and concentrate about heaven, and then hell. Hell is nothing like they say, and neither is heaven. In the darkness of the shitter it comes to me, though after I'm outside again I pretend I didn't think it, and discard the possibility as lunacy: heaven and hell are the same place.

A CHILD, A DREAM

Every other Sunday morning I drive up the highway toward the cape, through the Francis Marion National Forest with all the pine trees snapped a third of the way up from hurricane Hugo. Short, bushy trees are growing back now. The forest is dense down below with green, and speckled on top with tufts of green, and in between are the snapped trees. I look at the shacks along the way, and imagine what it must be like to live in them. I'm always imagining I'm someone else, with unusual peculiarities shaping my development. Sometimes I see a rusted tractor sitting in a yard and think of growing up with it there as an obstacle my whole carefree childhood, and how all things might be put in contrast or relation to the tractor. I'll see a shack with a billboard hovering like a tomcat over it, and I wonder what it would have done to my views of the world to have it looming over me every second of every day. I see big, wide fields of tobacco and I wonder if the tobacco in its various stages of growth would have instilled insecurities of some kind in me, or maybe just the opposite. People sit on their porches along the highway. They stare out at me, or intentionally ignore me. They wave, or toss accusatorial faces with a scratch to the back of the head, or tap of a bare foot on a porch rail. In early dawn the shacks glow with the sun behind them, like cobwebs in the grass. When I see them, I become senti-mental thinking of my days when fields were my playgrounds, and there were no barriers at least for an afternoon for a boy-atlas. My mind was boundless. I loved running in early morning fields, the dew dampening my jeans and downy skin. I was no amateur botanist, but merely an escapee. I moved without pause. My mind looped end-lessly like a waterwheel scooping and then dumping buckets of ob-servations about solitude, and solitude's stone and mortar. Now there is the toiling, which has replaced my time in the fields, and I am too weary to think too much of anything beyond my next drink, or break, or sandwich. The people in the shacks stare out with the same catatonic idiot stare I see when I look in the mirror at the end of the day.

Mrs. John Carpenter lives up the highway. John Carpenter used to work at the plastics factory. He taught me how to build fiberglass buoys. He died two years ago of a heart attack. He was only forty-two. Mrs. John Carpenter lives alone in her small two-bedroom shack, where she and John used to live together. They had a son, but the boy ran off three years ago to California. The boy writes Mrs. John Carpenter every now and then. She'll read me his letters over iced tea when I've finished the work. The boy is a homosexual. Mrs. John Carpenter doesn't know. I often wonder if John knew. John hated homosexuals. He hated homosexuals fiercely. He hated homo-sexuals, and he hated Chevy trucks and the people who drove them.

Mrs. John Carpenter does her laundry on Sundays. I mow the grass, and do any other odd job that she can't do herself, things John used to do. She has chickens, and two pigs. I like to feed them—both the chickens and pigs, I mean. I especially like the pigs. The pigs are cleaner than the chickens. It's quite a novelty for me, really. There's an old grindstone out back. When you turn the crank the stone goes around like a record left in the sun, except it's on its end and comes at you like a road. When it was new I bet the grindstone was something to marvel at, and whoever lived in the shack probably sharpened his tools more than he had to just so he could use it. The yard is wide, but not too deep because of the tobacco fields. While I'm pushing the mower across the yard, Mrs. John Carpenter is inside making me iced tea, or finishing a pie; then when I'm about half done she'll come out with her big wicker basket of clothes. When I've mowed beyond the clothesline, she'll begin hanging her clothes. She always wears dresses. Nothing fancy, but always smart. Her hair is shorter than I'd like, but from a distance it looks like it could be in a bun. I pretend it's in a bun, among other things. Mrs. John Carpenter makes me think of my mother. It's the way she snaps the sheets before pinning them up. There are moments when I feel strong attractions for her, and on more than one occasion I've fished for signs of weakness or loneliness, which I could use as a way of seducing her. But it's not because she resembles my mother that I have these fantasies. She makes me think of Jeanette. Jeanette, I knew, when I was six years old. She had ebullient red hair and freckles. We spent two summers together in backyard shade, and out on the open, urban streets, roaming and adventuring. After the summers with Jeanette it was a full ten years before I wanted any part of the female order again. I've been looking for her wherever I go, in every woman's face, and the closest I've come to finding her is in the person of Mrs. John Carpenter. There are times we're sitting on the picnic table, me with my shoulders hunched and sweaty hair plastered like tar to my scalp tonguing a glass of iced tea, and she sitting beside me on the same bench always listening with careful attentiveness, or reading me one of her son's letters—I'll catch myself about to refer to some childhood memory that we've shared together. My mouth opens. It's pitiful, and embarrassing. I'll quickly turn this lapse of spatial and temporal identity into a comment on the tobacco rows and their fine progress, or how good the iced tea feels on the back of my throat so good it gives me a headache. She really does remind me of my mother. I can't deny it. Who's going to lock me up for saying it? Jeanette, she was just an infantile version of my mother—why do you think I took to her? You think there weren't other girls in the neighborhood to play with? It was the way she wanted nothing from me. Even then, in sandboxes, girls wanted things that I didn't have, or couldn't obtain. But not Jeanette. She wanted nothing. The flakes of green paint at the edge of Mrs. John Carpenter's picnic table remind me of the rust on the old swing set; they remind me of peonies and ants and pounding the asphalt with a little hammer; they remind me of station wagons filled with wild children. Jeanette, with her dirty feet and pudgy fingers. Her missing teeth and kooky laugh.

"How's the pie?" Mrs. John Carpenter asked me.

"Mm-mm-*mm*," I said.

"Would you like another piece?"

"Oh, gosh," I said letting out the air in my lungs making a sound like a punctured tire.

"You'll have another piece," she smiled.

"I'll burst."

"You've only had two itty-bitty pieces. A workingman like you? Why, you're nothing but bones."

"Well," I said. "You know you make a mighty good elderberry pie, Mrs. Carpenter. You can't get elderberry pie just any place. Some people don't like it. It's too bitter, they say. It's too runny, they say. Hell, they don't know what they're missing. You save all the elderberry pie for me, and let them have the rest."

"Your wife doesn't make you pie?"

"Are you kidding?"

"A man needs good eating, if you want him to stay put."

Ballad of the Confessor

"Rhubarb pie, and elderberry pie. They'd make me stick around, all right. Tell me, Mrs. Carpenter, what was John's favorite?"

"His favorite pie?" she said, lifting an eyebrow and leaning back. "He liked elderberry, same as you." Mrs. Carpenter thought about it. I watched her, and listened, and while I did I scraped the dark berry filling from my plate. "Apple. Raspberry. Strawberry. There wasn't any pie John didn't consume rather quickly."

"I remember him at the shop. Everybody'd be done with their lunches sitting around the table, and then John would bring out a piece of your pie. A great big mouth-watering piece of pie. He'd sit there and eat it, real slow, torturing the rest of us."

"Dear," said Mrs. Carpenter. "He should have told me. I would have sent enough for all of you."

"I know you would have. The thing is, Mrs. Carpenter, you don't know how many guys down at the shop thought John was the luckiest guy in the world, all because of those pieces of pie. We all had sandwiches. You know, all the wives were sandwich makers; but that pie. I think you saved a fellow's job more than once with it. Made John a mellower sort of person. After lunch, he was real approachable. Me, I never had any trouble with John. That's because I understood him. You understand somebody, and then you don't take the rough edges so hard. Some of the other guys, there were times they didn't go for John's temper."

"He did have a temper," Mrs. Carpenter said, nodding her head in agreement. She tapped her lip.

"But the pie. He was a different man after it. I'm telling you—it's true. Men's jobs were saved. Families were held together. Children never knew how close they were to the brink of a miserable upbringing. Nobody makes pies anymore. Not the way you make them. Not the way my mom made them."

Mrs. John Carpenter left me, and I let my head drop back like my neck was broken. I wanted to feel the sun on my face. The sun is always glancing my face, all day long. It hits me at obtuse angles; it wears me out. . . I could feel it now scorching my skin. The two pieces of pie in my stomach, and the sun making mincemeat out of my already burnt face threw me into a mild delirium—it was then I had a half-dream. I'm all the time having half-dreams at work when me and Reggie take our breaks and sleep under the trees, or when I come home after work to get off my aching feet. I'm out in two minutes.

The half-dream at Mrs. John Carpenter's that day was clear and brilliant. I was in a dark place. It was so dark I can't say where it was. It began with music. The sound seemed to me something I knew before I heard it. There was a pronounced drumming. Yes, in fact the drumming was the dominant feature. The drumming resounded inside my chest, so that the beat shook me. The drumming beat evenly, with variations here and there, but never losing the central rhythm. I felt myself drifting into a very contented state. I've had this feeling before. I have it only when I'm dead tired, falling quickly asleep. It takes me without warning like an undertow. There are times I don't lose consciousness completely, I am aware of my free-wheeling mind, and it's here that I comprehend my own mortality. Death seldom frightens me. I can't imagine what death could offer that could be worse than perpetual weariness. But, here in this state, the finality of death hits me. It's terrifying. I think, my life is a third over, or near it—maybe more when you consider that time moves faster the older you get. In no time at all I'll be dead and buried. Fortunately, I dream about death only occasionally. More often I have a much different dream. The feeling is blissful, very familiar, yet indistinguishable. When I think too hard about it, it moves away from me. It seems to have a reason for being there, but wants to keep the reason hidden. In this most recent dream, the feeling was stronger than it had ever been. The drumming pounded throughout me in the most pleasant vibrations. As often is the case when the sensation has me, I was conscious of something. I thought that it might be a word. I don't know why it always attracts me first as an elusive word. I surround this unnamed thing with what seems to be a large set of hands. I believe they are my hands, if they're hands at all. When these hands get close to the word-thing, the feeling of excitation in my chest is heightened, it's as though I'm approaching some new ecstasy. In my latest half-dream, for the first time, I saw the word-thing. Suddenly, there it was before me, unveiled, clear, and the instant I saw it I knew it couldn't have been anything else: The word was *You*. But the thing that *You* represented was not the normal thing it represents—it was a mulberry tree. The mulberry tree was the one I knew as a youth—the giant old tree along the dirt lane. The base of the trunk was hollowed out on one side, and I remember being frightened that a raccoon lived inside the trunk and would rush out at us at any moment. We picked berries from the lower branches and put them in our shirts pulled out and wished we were birds so we could reach higher where most of the berries were. In my half-dream, it made perfect sense. It's confusing to me now. It takes concentration to get through the confusion to the core of meaning, but I can do it. I was able to look directly at the word-tree without it moving away. My hands descended on it, and when I held it my hands were like leaves or roots, and they absorbed its energy. When I held it as the tree, all things seemed to be illuminated with golden light. When I held it as the word, *You*, more of my mind was triggered, and without my trying I was aware, simultaneously, of its careless uses. I knew what even now I cannot fully comprehend, though I can describe what I knew—that the meaning of *You* is meaningless. It's meaningless when attached to the walking dead. It's meaningless in the artificial and traitorous laws written by unimaginative cowards. Its spotlight is false, reducing men to heroes and villains—first lie in the Book of Lies.

The half-dream, like any other, mutated into another. I saw Mrs. John Carpenter floating in a purple sky, wearing a white lace gown. At first I thought she was a cloud. She moved across the purple sky touching stars as they passed, and as she touched them they burned in white-orange light, brilliantly, then glowed a more muted orange after she was gone. Mrs. John Carpenter was so beautiful. Ahead of her was an array of stars, and behind her was a trail of glowing orange hands. I noticed then that Mrs. John Carpenter was weeping. I wanted to weep with her. I wanted to float next to her. I wanted to stop time and freeze her there so I could possess her. Then, she split into a thousand points of light. She seemed to have passed through some unseen sieve in the purple sky, and her body on the other side was not crushed, but strained, duplicated, and reborn. Her thousand new selves sprayed out across eternity like a geyser.

THE HYPNOTIC LURE
OF EVIL

Boog works part-time; I never really understood his situation. I'll see him for a few days in a row, then won't see him for a week. He's maybe fifty, but looks a lot older. The skin on his forearms, which are always bare from his short-sleeve, Howdy Doody shirts, is scorched with sunspots. His face and neck are all gritty and plastery looking, a little lumpy. He's big. Tall big and big-handed, big-boned. His head is big like a block of concrete. He has a stoop to him, and when you're close by you're in his shadow. His voice comes out like an old locomotive, though he rarely raises it very much higher than a steady *chug-a-chug*. All the time he's got his hands inside the front of his too tight jeans, or in his back pockets. When his hands are in his back pockets, his elbows stick out like plucked chicken wings. He wanders through the nursery carrying flats for the girls, and if you didn't know he was an employee you'd think he was just some friendly customer lending a hand. He helps out with loading cars, or fetching bags of soil or manure when me and Reggie aren't around. His presence can't be missed, but at times he just falls back into the dense foliage and swirls of dust.

His wife left him some years ago. You wouldn't think it bothers him because of his leathery skin and unsympathetic, blood-shot eyes, but it does. He drinks a lot, and it's his wife that he's trying to forget or remember at the strip joints and crummy seaside dives. He used to be somebody. Mitch says he used to work at the water treatment plant up near Orangeburg. He was the head guy. Mitch had a friend who worked for him part time. The friend said Boog was about the meanest bastard he'd ever met. He was the dog Boog had for beating. Every day he'd greet him in the morning with a "Hey, Bigfoot, why don't you clean off your boots before you come in here. Look at the way you're tromping dirt in here. Didn't your mother ever teach you how to act? Damn Yankee. Damn Minnesota Bigfoot." Then, turning to the two regular employees, he'd talk about him as if he wasn't there. "You guys ever been to Minnesota? Nothing but a cesspool. Every God damn person I ever met from that state's been nothing but a dirty, lazy bum. Don't know why they don't use the place as a big trash heap. We should send all our trash up there, to Minnesota, and dump it starting in the middle and work our way out. I'll be God damned if it ain't the worst place in the world. Worse than Puerto Rico. Worse than China. Worse than Russia. How it ever got to be let into the union, hell if I know." Boog was from Illinois. He talked all the time about Yankees like he'd been born and raised in the South. Boog gave Mitch's friend every demeaning job he could find. He made him clean the toilets without a brush, using only rubber gloves. He made him mow the grass where there was no reason to mow it, where he knew there might be snakes or fire ants. For two weeks he made him sit in the sun breaking old water meters with a hammer to extract the copper so he could sell it to the scrap yard. He didn't really need the help, but the budget allowed for an extra part-timer and Boog wasn't about to let go of his whipping boy. Mitch's friend said there were times he wanted to throw himself on Boog and pop his eyes out, or rip out his balls. He'd never done anything to elicit the abuse; it came from the depths of Boog's razor wire soul. To make matters worse, Mitch's friend depended on Boog for a ride to work each morning. He had no car. Boog never spoke to him as they drove to work. The silence was another form of intentional, calculated abuse. After work Boog and the two regulars stopped at the carryout and got some beer and stood leaning over the sides of his pickup drinking and tossing the cans in with the hoses and pumps and shovels and sand. Mitch's friend had no choice but to tag along. He had no money for beer. He couldn't spare fifty cents. The two regulars knew he had no money, it was obvious from the holes in his boots, and the ketchup sandwiches he had sometimes for lunch, and how whenever he walked past the vending machines at work his eyes would react as if there was a nude woman standing beside him. Boog, when he bought the beer, might say to him, "Bigfoot, go ahead and have a beer if you want." He'd say it the way you might drop a steak bone to a dog. Sometimes he was more direct about his resentment: "How come you never buy, Bigfoot? You're always drinking our beer, but you never buy. God damn mooch. That's what you are. A mooch from the great piss-hole state of Minnesota."

Mitch admitted later on that his friend was really him, but that he was too ashamed to say so in the beginning. He said Boog's wife left him because he treated her like a frying pan, he was just plain mean to her, the way he was mean to him. She left him before, more than once, but this time it was final. Boog couldn't let go of his meanness. Mitch said there was something about Boog that made you pity him, even though he was so mean.

"I can't look at him too long," Mitch said once. "It's like seeing yourself in old photographs, or re-reading old love letters. It's not something a body can stomach, for fear of seeing yourself."

One day me and Reggie and Mitch and Boog were unloading a

shipment of pine straw. Pine straw comes from this guy who brings it in an old school bus. All the windows are broken out. The guy who drives the bus does no manual labor. He has two laborers, one middle-aged and another very old, who drop the bales on the ground at the back of the bus. The old laborer moves in a sleep walk. I expect him to keel over any minute. The inside of the bus with its floating pine straw dust must feel twice as hot as it is for us beneath the open sun. The thought's occurred to me to jump up and help them out, but I never have. The two laborers don't ever talk to us. They cough and sneeze from the pine straw dust, but only stop to take water when all the pine straw has been unloaded. Then they sit inside the bus sipping water, their greasy hair lightened with dust and their heads sparkling like stream pebbles from sweat, each staring in different directions. Before this, while we were still moving bales, me and Boog were walking together, him first then me. Boog moved slowly so I would always be right behind him. He was telling me about God, the natural order of things, and the one colossal truth he's learned in life.

". . . When you get down to it, that's what they are. They can't help it, same as we can't help it. But you can't deny it. You know the plagues they talk about in the Bible? What they're really talking about are cunts. That's the plague. I'm telling you. Every human problem can be traced back to that small piece of real estate. All life comes from it. All movement on earth is directed in either trying to obtain it, or trying to get rid of it. God isn't a man. You think Jesus was a man? What I mean is, if you accept what I've said about cunts, then it explains why Jesus was so deferential toward women. It's because God is a woman. She is. And Jesus was Her Phil Donahue. It explains everything. It explains why Jesus liked the poor. It explains why He helped the sick. It explains why He forgave the scum of the earth. Only a mother, or at least a woman, thinks like that. I hate to admit it, but that's our Maker. She's a smart one. Instead of making Him in Her own image, She made Him in the image of a man. You think any man who's a real man would go for a *Daughter* of God? She knew better. The apostles, I think they figured it out. But they were afraid to say anything about it. They left us clues though. Who was the one who betrayed Jesus? Who was it? Judas. That's him. He knew. That's what he was really trying to say. 'Hey everybody—this guy's a phony. This guy's really a—' Silenced. You never hear about the guys who wrote the Old Testament, because they were all castrated and sent to eternal damnation. They tried to tell it like it was. They showed us how Eve was. They told us about the plagues— cunts, in other words. They talked about the wrath of God, meaning the wrath of woman. Even they had to camouflage it some. But if you accept on faith the original premise, that God is a woman, then everything else falls into place. It's clear as water."

"You really believe that?" I said weakly, not wanting to get sucked into a real conversation.

"What do you mean, do I really believe it?" Boog said with big-boned, macho surprise.

It's a good thing I was so tired; I might have killed him. "We think it's hot out here," I said to nobody in particular, nodding to the laborers in the bus. I was becoming delirious from fatigue.

"Don't you believe it?" Boog said.

"I think it's just about the biggest pile of crap I've ever heard," I told him.

You could see him seething by the rapid, repetitive clenching of his teeth. From then on we worked separately. It wasn't long after that Boog began following Mitch around. I heard them talking. Soon, they were hooting and laughing. A short while later, Boog was ahead of Mitch, and Mitch was following him. Boog did most of the talking then, and Mitch, who would not look me in the eyes now, wore a glossy-eyed, idiot-grin. I wondered about that grin. We were passing each other, when suddenly I thrust my hand out toward him and took hold of his arm. He yanked his arm free. We glared at each other. The sharper my eyes drilled into him, the sharper his became. Boog sauntered behind him, whistling toward the sky, and when he got to the pile of pine straw at the rear of the bus he began laughing, mockingly. I knew he was laughing at me. Mitch, who was watching Boog, turned back toward me. His idiot-grin turned into a silent form of Boog's mockery.

"Mitch," I said.

"Coon-lover," he answered.

"What did you say?"

"You heard me."

It took me a moment to understand his meaning. A gush of anguish passed through me. I saw Mitch's eyes move deliberately over to Reggie and the bus driver, who were sitting on pine straw bales beneath some trees, then back to me.

I went to say something. I lifted my hand. It shook. My arm shook. My whole body shook. I went to tell him things, but all that came out was a grotesque croak, a feeble utterance as though I had been shot in the stomach. I felt his gaze as I became small, and cowardly. My cowardice, the full, plump cowardice that raised its head that day at that moment, is known only to him, and to Boog. It is not even fully known to them, for they view it I'm sure not as cowardice, but fear. Fear of them, fear of involvement. They're right. I was and am afraid. Fear is what made me pause; cowardice is what made me stand still. There, rendered mute and incapable of defiance, I lost hope of becoming a great man. We all think ourselves great men. That possibility was shredded in an instant. Reggie has not discovered it. He knows nothing of that day. Mitch and Boog act no differently toward him, and perversely, no differently toward me. Reggie

Ballad of the Confessor

and I sit sleeping on trees during break, share secrets big and small inside the shitter, go fishing on odd Saturdays; he doesn't know. More than the pain of my act, is the pain from his ignorance. He would probably understand. He's not one to confront people himself—there's every reason in the world to believe he would have done the same thing. Maybe he has. The prospect gives me hope. Hope that all of humanity is as cowardly as me. What kind of man hopes for such a thing?

The moment came and then went. It came unexpectedly and unsolicited. Part of me feels unfairly targeted—I believe that I am no different from those I see around me, yet they are spared from spiritual dissection merely because they have not been presented this plain, stark choice. Their cowardice remains hidden behind the shroud of disuse. I feel stricken with some shameful disease, removed from others not by my makeup, but by fate. Yet, the fact remains, I *am* different. My act of betrayal was epic. It wasn't some harmless slight Mitch, in his own considerable fatigue, had blurted out, blundered, as we all blunder from time to time. It was the budding of evil that stood before me, and I chose to let it pass.

ALONG HISTORY'S ROAD

"The only reason he ain't in for rape," Reggie said to me, "is 'cause he's got powers over the girl."

"What do you mean, *powers?*"

"I mean, well, she don't wanna be known as a whore, and if she was to come out with it, it'll all come out. She don't want that."

"Is she a whore?"

"She's got a need for it, and it don't necessarily matter who's there to satisfy it."

"Was she hurt bad?"

"Son," Reggie said, "he raped her. Don't you know what that means?"

"I meant, did he beat her up."

"Didn't beat her up. Wasn't like that."

"How was it?"

"They been having sex. They were regular partners. He's married, you know. Well, one night he comes over and he don't wanna use a rubber. She always made sure he used a rubber. So, she says I don't want you then, you'll have to just leave. But he says he still wants to, just without no rubber. She tells him, 'Leave, get off a me.' But he won't leave. Next thing you know, he's forcing his way in, and she can't do nothing about it. And that's how he raped her."

"How long ago was it?"

"Oh, maybe a year and a half, I think."

"How'd you find out?"

"She told me herself. Not exactly the way I told you. It explains a lot. But then, it starts me thinking too."

"Like what?"

We were looking for worms under the five-gallon crepe myrtles. It rained the day before. The mulch was the perfect dampness beneath the containers, and the worms, thinking they were safe between the fibrous roots, were stunned when they were seized and dropped into a coffee can.

"Makes me think about daughters, and mothers. And wives. It's a sad thing when your daughter's a whore. I think of my daughter getting raped like Roxy. I think, what makes a girl turn into a whore? I think I know, but maybe I don't. I've known lots of whores. I wonder, does she like it, being what she is, I mean? I don't think she does. But then I think she does. I think she does, and she doesn't. She does, or she wouldn't do it. She doesn't, because she told me so. Just because she does, doesn't mean she likes it, I suppose. What do you think?"

"You know who the guy was?"

"I do," Reggie said. "But I ain't sayin'."

"I don't want you to say. I just wondered if you knew. When I think about him, I get worked up inside. I like Roxy. She's a nice girl. I don't care if she is a whore; it doesn't mean she's not a nice girl. I think about him doing that to her. It makes me want to do something. I don't know what I want to do, but I want to do something. But you know what? It makes me sacred too."

"What you be scared for?"

"I'm scared of how much of him is in me."

"You think you could ever do what he done?" Reggie said to me. He was breathing not hard, but steady, and sweat rolled down his cheeks. His glasses held no glare in them because of the clouds, and I could see his eyes.

"I know I could," I said.

"You're honest."

"Maybe I'm dangerous."

"Maybe. But you're honest. That makes you less dangerous."

"You think I'm like him?"

"Naw," Reggie said dismissively. "You really ain't nothing like him."

"Reggie," I said. "What if you don't want to be something, but you are anyway; what happens to people like that?"

"What happens when?"

"When you die. You think there's any hope of going to heaven?"

He shrugged. "Beats me."

"I have thoughts," I said. "I have these thoughts, see."

"Son, I don't need to hear 'em."

"You don't wanna hear 'em?"

"No, I ain't sayin' I don't wanna hear 'em. What I'm saying is, you don't need to tell me if you really don't wanna tell me."

"But I do wanna tell you. I have to maybe. Nobody else will listen without thinking I'm pure evil." I just went ahead then. "I have thoughts, see, and I can't seem to stop 'em. Other people might have boundaries around their thoughts, keeping them a certain way. But I don't have any boundaries. I don't have any at all. All kinds of bad thoughts enter my head. I can't help it. I don't know where they come from. All kinds of good thoughts enter my head too. All kinds of thoughts of every kind. There's no filter. There's no stop sign. It's what makes me scared."

Ballad of the Confessor

"If you're scared, it's good."

"You think I've ever done some really bad things?"

"Sure," said Reggie.

"I have."

"I know."

"You know?"

"What, you think I'm stupid?"

"I'm not saying what. And I'm not saying I do most of what I think sometimes. But, I'm not who you think I am."

"Trouble with you, son," Reggie said putting his big bear paw on my shoulder, "is you think too much."

"Why do you think I'm not like him?"

"Oh," Reggie said jiggling his can looking down in at his catch. "Maybe you are. Maybe I don't really know you very much."

"I'm telling you," I said shaking my head.

"You ain't nothing like him really. You got nothing to worry about."

"Some day I might bust. The cap might come off. I'm scared."

"Aw," Reggie said. "The world can handle it."

"You think so? I'm just a faker."

"Naw," he said. "You ain't a faker. You just ain't got nowhere to turn."

I was standing at the card display in Food Lion, looking at birthday cards. Every one of those cards looked phony, and I was staring at them watching them get phonier and phonier. I don't ever send birthday cards. I hate cards. I hate getting them. I hate sending them. I was standing in front of the toothpaste. All I wanted was regular toothpaste. There was every kind under the sun, except regular toothpaste. It's the same when you're looking for cream cheese, or cold medicine, or coffee. There's too many choices. Some day I'd like to take a tube of tartar control minty whitening toothpaste and

116

squeeze it up one of those marketing asshole's asshole. Marketing assholes are ruining the world one product at a time. I was in the milk section for five minutes, staring at the organic milk. People buy that stuff like it's nothing. I get the Food Lion brand. I get the Food Lion brand of milk, cheese, sugar, toilet paper, and bread. Some day I'll be able to buy organic milk. I dream about it in the middle of the night. When I say I dream about it, I mean I wake up and think about it. I wonder what it tastes like. I bet it tastes real smooth like a vanilla milk shake. I bet you can feel the purity sliding past your throat. I think about the organic cows that make the organic milk; they must be the happiest cows around. I bet they're living the good life on some Swiss-looking hillside right out of the set of *Heidi*. Bells clinking, farts echoing through the valleys. Nobody's shooting them up with steroids and fucking with their DNA. Jesus. My body's full of things I can't even pronounce, mixed up by some cave-dwelling scientist who wants to make a name for himself crossing a grasshopper with a sequoia. I wish just once I could afford to buy a half-gallon of that organic milk. I'm being killed with every swallow, but there's nothing I can do about it. They say you can't drive without your seat belt on, but it's okay to put ego experiments in milk. Why are people afraid of the Unabomber and not the government? I wonder if the lady in the Capri pants and NASCAR T-shirt knows what I'm thinking. I wonder if that camera can read my thoughts. She's got the organic milk in her cart. Organic milk, organic spinach, and Pepperidge Farm bread. She won't even look at me. Why won't she look at me? What's the matter with me? I'm dirty, but there's nothing wrong with me. I'm just dirty, can't you see? After a shower, I'll look just like anybody else. Pretty much like anybody else. Why won't you just look up and smile at me? I'm human. I could be your brother. I could be your father. I could be your son. I don't understand.

Ballad of the Confessor

On the way home my shoulders got tired from carrying the bags. I had to stop. I was afraid to stand in one place too long for fear of the fire ants. People blared their horns at me. I barely hear them anymore. Some of the Gullah women were set up under their canopies weaving baskets. They drive mini-vans—all of them—so they can haul their baskets back and forth from wherever they live to the side of the road along the highway. I rested under one lady's canopy and she didn't seem to mind, but she didn't seem to not mind. She watched me every third or fourth weave. I don't know what she thought I was going to do standing there with two armfuls of food. I didn't think I made a very threatening figure, but who knows? At the next canopy the woman from Food Lion was there. I slowed down. The woman stood in sandals, her feet and calves brown and smooth and tempting. She stretched up on her toes examining baskets that hung from the canopy. The Gullah woman frowned at me when I came along dragging my groceries. I went around her canopy. She said something to me, but I don't follow Gullah too good. It made it easy to ignore her. When I was going past the Food Lion woman, I caught an eyeful. I swerved my head over and there was her ass puckered in the middle by the Capri pants that were too tight. I stared long and hard. I felt like I was stealing something, and she couldn't stop me. Nobody could stop me. The Gullah woman jabbered at me. I ignored her. I was outside her canopy. She couldn't stop me. Nobody could stop me. The woman in the Capri pants didn't know what I was taking from her, and doing to her. It didn't matter that I didn't do it for real. I did it. I took it. The Gullah woman bore witness. Nothing can stop eyes, or thoughts. At least nothing yet.

When I was close to home, I stopped again. My arms and shoulders were on fire. There was no shade. I stood surrounded by debris from the cars that went by, in a wasteland of grass struggling to blanket the recently graded berm. I looked down at a two-litre plastic bottle. I looked at the new asphalt curb. My mind went into a tailspin. I closed my eyes. I heard the cars clearly then. I became aware that I could no longer feel my arms or shoulders. I saw Roxy. She took on the missing feeling of my arms and shoulders. The two sides of her floated around me, and I waited as though she were a plane wanting to land. Images flashed like strobes in the darkness, of Roxy sitting outside the trailer under the awning, staring past customers, flicking her pen in manic diversion; then frames of her body in tight skirts and open blouses. I jumped up, waving for her to come home and reconnect to my body. She shied from coming closer. Then, more flashes. Grotesque, dirty images of Roxy being assaulted—I saw only the back of the man, his spine clenching and releasing beneath taut skin, and Roxy's face, her eyes opened in bewilderment more than fear or pain. Her eyes replaced the two halves of my missing limbs; they grew into mammoth spheres that pressed against me heavy and damp. The pressure crushed me, and brought me to the point of crying out. I felt my head caving in. The sound of the assaults throbbed around the severed points near my missing shoulders. The two spheres drifted into the blackness. There was nothing but the two spheres throbbing, now circling each other. As they moved they ripped the blackness, leaving behind them fantastic sparks of the most brilliant colors; the points of color floated away like leaves on an autumn river. I found myself circling, circling. My whole purpose seemed to be contained in my movement around the other sphere, in our unspoken interdependence and need. The distance between us diminished, but not as fast as I wanted. It was torturous being always in the other's sight, yet unable to join with it. I felt myself letting go, but then because there was no other way, no other life that I knew, I recovered from the lapse with a more ardent hope and concentration.

Ballad of the Confessor

I opened my eyes. I was standing in a field of faded cornhusks. It was winter and the rows of harvested corn were beautiful, they were perfect in their order and pattern. I lifted my arms, opened my mouth, and the snow that was falling began clinging to my face, and to the husks resting silent after their summer flourish. I opened my eyes. I was surrounded by beautiful gypsies. They touched me with tickling caresses and kissed me with lips moist and full, and I fell into a heady dream standing among them the center of everything. I felt repulsed by my own hesitation and suddenly I began to vomit this hesitation, and out came spectrums of not just color, but sound, smell, taste, touch, want, hope, disease, war, denial. I opened my eyes, it was no dream this time. I saw the cars from the corner of my eye; I heard blares and obscenities. I saw in the sky billows of white, and at the far range of my vision in either direction my fingertips pointing to the heavens like hopeful, miniature towers. There was a breeze. It came from the north, and as I lowered my head and looked down to the long stretch of highway studded on either side with Gullah women and their canopies flapping like Phoenician sails, cars streaking like monsters in medieval tapestries, and the simple, easy swaying of the trees showing their upturned leaves in that familiar signal of oncoming rain, there came puffs of white from the cottonwoods. The sky was alive with opaque escape-clusters parading toward me. For a moment I dwelt in the arms of God.

BALLAD OF THE MISBEGOTTEN

The pier is old, older than anything. I went there one night not long ago. I know those who come out at night on the pier; the sacred fishermen come out at night. These men gather on the moving boards to flee what chases them, or to search for the big prize. (Always there is a breeze on the pier, but the breeze when it brings the plump summer swelter is nothing but a mute songbird.) These men drink, oh they drink. Their coolers come full of ice and beer, and leave with less ice and less beer, and perhaps if they are lucky, a fish or two. (There are bats all around—above the lights—swooping down across the pier, appearing then disappearing.) These men tend to obsess. It's their obsessions that gutted marriages, alienated children, lost jobs; but in their youth the obsessions flung them through streaking years of immortality, then long stretches of humbled servitude blotted with dripping, weeping pages of whoredom and aggressions. (The pier is never still. It moves. The movement is something you get used to, or, if not, will turn you away and return you to your source of childhood purgatory. The smell of fish clings like diamond studs to the wooden pier; the guts of cut bait smears hands and the fronts of jeans.) I've seen emotions that have no

121

Ballad of the Confessor

known names in our English language arise, like new butterflies, here on these warped boards. It's no place for prudes, priests, or politicians. Frontier democracy as a political scheme may be dead, but here on the pier it's the one and only governor of our invisible island. You are fairly, silently ranked by how well your cut mullet stays on its hook, how far you can cast, and your percentage of catches to hits. This ranking has meaning—for it determines your tone of voice, your seated posture, your eye contact, and how often you are permitted to contribute to conversations about everything and nothing. Upon the sluggish summer air, our conversations joust with great ideas and tragic deeds. Across the land men sit huddled toward one another in similar pods, in similar places, and the miracle of peasant fortitude orates to the vastness of the galaxy.

"Jesus Christ," says a voice, weighted with disgust.

"He-he-he."

"You're one sick bastard."

"He-he-he. Spaghetti and hot sausage," the second voice says, momentarily able to speak only in broken sentences through the laughter. "Always gets me going."

"Well, don't shit your pants."

"He-he-he." The second one, who's name is Billy, leans to the side and rips another, this one not silent like the first, but bold, sending not-so-unpleasant-sounding reverberations against the wooden bench. Everybody stands clear.

"You sick mother fucker," a third voice, Pete, says waving his hand against the oncoming odor.

"Hey. . . he-he-he. . . I can't help it," Billy laughs.

"Go in and wipe your ass," Pete tells him. "Go on. You filthy fuck."

"I. . . I. . . think I'm all done," says Billy. "That was the big one."

"Man," says Pete. "How can you live with yourself."

122

"I don't know," Billy shrugs.

"Billy, if you weren't such a good waitress, I'd throw you to the sharks," says the first voice. His name is Perry. Perry, who last year caught a seven-foot shark up on Garret's pier. Perry, who was not alone at the time, but because his brother and brother-in-law were passed out drunk in the truck, hauled in the creature by himself. Perry, who by virtue of that single act of foolishness, was revered as a legend.

"Go get me a beer," says Big Tex. Big Tex two years ago lost balance walking over the parking lot to his car; he fell on top of me and tore up my knee. I couldn't walk for three days, and then limped around for the next two months.

"You got one already," Billy answers him.

"Go get me a beer, Billy," Big Tex repeats.

"But you got one. I just saw you open it."

"Billy," says Perry, nodding towards Big Tex's cooler. That was all Perry had to say.

While Billy went over to the cooler, Pete tossed a bloodworm on his bench. He took another one and held it over Billy's beer, his eyes looking to Perry for the okay. Perry, whose wild hair sat atop a balding scalp like a clump of weeds, his eyes looking out like big billiard balls from behind his thick glasses, gave a hurried nod no. Billy came back and sat right down on the bloodworm. We fought to control ourselves.

"What?" Billy said. "What?"

"Nothing," I said.

"What'd you do?" Billy said looking around.

"We didn't do nothing," Pete said

"Yes, you did. I know you did."

Billy stood up. "What?" The bloodworm stuck to the wrinkled seat of his pants. Big Tex, who had the best view, shook his head and chuckled, his big beer gut moving like shifting cargo beneath his taut shirt.

"Why're you laughing?" Billy looked at Big Tex.

"Petey just told a joke."

"No he didn't. Come on; what is it?"

"Billy," Perry said standing up and going over to check his line, "you fart one more time and, well, we'll see." Perry flicked the butt of his cigarette out into the darkness. Billy walked over to him and asked him what they did. The bloodworm was beginning to fall away from his pants. Everybody watched, cheering silently for the bloodworm in its vain attempt to cling to Billy's ass.

Billy is only twenty years old. His father had no dog to beat, so he beat Billy verbally with insults, the froth of his own self-hatred. Every day his father compared him to his neighbor's boy, who was a running back on the football team, and one of the more popular students. "Why can't you be like *him*?" his father would say. Of course, his father was really asking himself the question, a lamentation of his own deficiencies and failures. This, he hid in the easy ridicule of his own son. Billy tried all through school to be something, to impress his father. It consumed him. He became focused on it; everything else was clutter in contrast to this single desperate desire to gain his father's approval. The more his father criticized him, the more it fueled his desire. The boy had two older brothers. They had been athletes. Billy was a mistake. The first two were mistakes, but not of the magnitude that Billy was a mistake. He came five years after the second brother, when his father was already contemplating his mediocre life. His father did not possess the guiltlessness required to abandon his family, so he remained as a foreigner in his own household, finding occasional comfort in the two older boys, and abusing his wife and Billy. Billy's mother had been popular with both the boys and girls as a youth. Her own father was a stranger who spent weeks away as a train conductor. When he was home, he ruled the house with impatience and cruelty. He had incestuous relations with her. Billy's father discovered the secret one night while they were walking a country lane, and it enraged him to such a degree that he took a stone and began hitting himself in the foot with it. Billy's mother wept, running down the lane, her life surely ruined by her divulgence. Billy's father, as he lay in bed looking out his window to the subtle bend of the maple leaves, vowed to protect Susan, his girl. It was protection, and not love, then, that was the impetus on his part toward marriage. For her part, Susan accepted this affection, which to her at the age of sixteen seemed like love in its most passionate, and glorious manifestation.

The epic mistake led to a life of unhappiness for Billy's father and mother, and for the first eighteen years of his life, for Billy. He left home upon graduation, spent a year at college, and found work that following summer with a traveling carnival. Carnival life suited him for a while. He liked the steady, ever-changing supply of gullible teenaged girls, who were attracted to the most lecherous and pathetic of men. Billy often wondered about it. He came to the conclusion that girls were naturally attracted to lechery; it allowed them to experience, through the opposite sex, perversions, risks, and baseness denied to females by the rules of The Game. The carnival, because of its brevity, allowed them to shed the normal guilt and denial of their urges. He often pitied the girls he slept with, even while making love to them. They told him stories that are never told anywhere else. He became a hater of his own sex, and then a hater of himself. He wished for purity, and honor, and this is what made him leave the carnival last September. But the carnival did not leave him. He had become addicted to the revolving supply of young flesh. His thoughts were consumed with images of girls sprawled on backs in the throes of ecstasy. This has become his obsession. He is here on the pier in some vague attempt to shed himself of it.

The others don't know about Billy, except that he was with the carnival and decided to jump off when it came to Charleston. He's a poor fisherman, but they like his stories. He's a surrogate son to the men who fish the pier at night. He's a magic carpet for those who've forgotten what sweet-smelling tender love was like, or for those who never knew. Life is lived through him, so that the fruit of their real lives languish and wither from neglect.

"Billy," said Big Tex, "tell us about the mom." Big Tex is so large he can lean back and put his elbows on the railing.

"Ooh, yeah," said Pete. "That's a good one."

Perry, who had finished checking his line, sat back down on his cooler. "You sure you ain't making these up?" he said.

"Honest," Billy said, raising his hand. "I swear, I'm not making nothing up."

"Go ahead, Billy," said Big Tex.

"Aw, you don't wanna hear that," Billy said.

"Yeah, I do. Come on, Billy, tell it again."

"But you've heard it a dozen times."

"Twice. You only told it twice. Just once more."

"I know I've told it at least four times."

"Twice," Big Tex said authoritatively.

"Why don't *you* tell a story?" Billy said. "I bet you got lots of good stories."

"Billy, all my stories have been buried, if I had any to begin with. Now tell the mom story, or I'll push this bloodworm up your ass." Big Tex held a bloodworm in his fat fingers and showed it to him.

"Was she really, you know," said Pete, who whenever Billy told his stories found excuses to rearrange the front of his pants.

"I told you she was," said Billy. "Nobody thinks that with moms, but it's true. At least with her it was."

"And how many times she come to your tent for it?"

"Three straight nights, and one afternoon don't forget."

"Come on," Pete said, scooting toward the edge of his seat, making small panting sounds. "Please, Billy. A true blonde? A true blonde, you said?"

"Unless she colored it."

"Come on, Billy, tell it to us. It's the best story you got. It's the best story I ever heard, from you or anybody else. And to think, it's true."

Billy picked at a piece of dried fish guts stuck to his bench. I felt sorry for him, but I wanted to hear the mom story like the others. Billy didn't tell the mom story that night. He mistook vicariousness for empathy, and so he told us something else, something he never should have told us.

"This one," he began, "is better."

"We want the *mom* story," Pete whined.

"Let him tell it," Perry said. "Let the kid tell his story."

"He says it's better, Pete," said Big Tex. He shrugged his massive shoulders. "Who knows?"

Billy waited until all eyes and ears were turned toward him. He took out his fillet knife from its sheath, gripped it tightly so the tendons on the back of his hands showed through like the skeleton of an umbrella; he stabbed at the bleached plank between his legs as he told the story.

"There was this girl. I forget her name now. She was sixteen. She was nice, sweet. We hit it off right away. I was hot for her, but I liked her. She was the first girl I'd met in a long time that I thought maybe she could be my girl. It couldn't happen, but I thought about it anyway. I thought maybe we could date, and then who knows?"

"Blonde, brunette?" Pete asked.

"She was a brunette."

127

Ballad of the Confessor

"Big tits?"

"Medium to big."

"How tall?"

"Short. Just right, really. Anyway, that's not the point. She came to my tent one night, just like any of the others; but with her it was different. I wanted to be nice to her, to treat her nice, you know. She wasn't like the others. We stayed up all night—"

"That's my boy," said Pete.

"No." Billy frowned. "I mean, yeah, we sort of fooled around a little. But mostly we talked. I don't know. Part of me wanted the same thing I always wanted, and part of me wanted to be good to her, to protect her. I can't say for sure, but maybe I loved her. I don't know if I did or not, it sure seemed like it. We weren't together that long. The next day she came around to the booth looking so pretty. She wore a red tube top, and had her hair in a ponytail. Her cheeks were pink from walking the fair in the sun. She leaned over the booth and gave me a kiss when nobody was looking. Her face was warm and moist from the heat and she smelled so good. She hung around for a while, then went off with her friends. She came back a couple times and brought me things to eat. As I was sitting there on my stool, eating my french fries watching her walk away with her friends, I was happier than I've ever been. That's when I first began to think about what I was doing in the carnival. Suddenly, I felt I had to escape from it. It was like I'd had this pressure between my eyes blinding me, and I didn't even know it. It was like the pressure just stopped, and there it was everything easy for me to see.

"She came to my tent again that night. We left the carnival and walked around the park there. We sat near the pond back in the bushes and made out for about two hours. She said she knew the people who were making the candied apples and asked if I wanted to go see them. We went back to the carnival. We held hands all the way back. I felt like I was floating on a cloud. Everybody sat around outside, some people sticking the apples with wooden sticks, and some people dipping them in the candied apple goop. It wasn't just her friends there, but everybody from the carnival was lending a hand. People were drinking, smoking. Don't ever eat candied apples at a carnival; Jesus, there're some dirty people involved. What they say about carnies is true: some are running from the law, some are running from wives, some are hooked on drugs, some are just plain derelicts. I can't say I was any better than any of them, but that's how it is. There was this guy. I hardly noticed him at first. He was sitting off to the side behind the trashcan; just a smallish, frail little guy. He hardly said anything. Well, later on everybody left, after all the candied apples were made, and it was just me and the girl and the guy. She was good friends with him. Maybe they were related, I never found out. The two of them start talking, and pretty soon I figure out that the guy's got AIDS. She's asking him about his medicine, how he's been feeling and all that. The guy talked real low and weak. His hair was stubbly. He had white, sick skin. I didn't want to get near him. Then I start thinking about the apples. All the apples he made. I thought of all those people who wouldn't know what kind of sick bastard had made their candied apples. I don't think you can get AIDS from eating an apple, but who knows? Maybe you can. And anyway, even if you can't, the thought of it made me sick.

"The girl left. She just wandered off into the darkness and didn't come back. I thought she had to go to the bathroom or something, but she didn't come back. Meanwhile, I sat there with this guy. I didn't know what to say to him. I don't think he knew what to say to me either. We started making small talk. I had trouble hearing him. He was telling me about the roses that he grew. He said he used to work in his garden every day, but now he couldn't. He said his roses were being neglected. He said it killed him to think of his roses all dying.

"I was tired, dead tired. It must have been four in the morning. All I wanted to do was go back to my tent and sleep. But I fell asleep right where I was, in the lawn chair. I woke up. The birds were singing; it was almost morning. I looked over, and the guy had his head back, his mouth hung open wide. Somehow I knew it wasn't right. He didn't seem to be moving. I told him it was time to get up, but he didn't move. I shook him by the shoulder, but he still didn't move. Then I shook him a little harder. Nothing. I thought, maybe the guy's dead. He looked it. I told him—"Hey! Buddy! You all right?" The guy didn't flinch. It didn't look like he was breathing. I knew that if he was dead there was no hurry to tell anybody. He didn't have anybody who would have cared. I sat and stared at his face, and his little, shrunken body. He was the sickest-looking guy you'd ever want to see. Bony, hardly any flesh to him. Pale. Scrawny, just scrawny. I wondered what he looked like before. He probably looked a whole lot different."

Billy got up. He walked to the railing and stared out across the water. We all looked at each other, and asked each other with our eyes, *What's he going to do?* He turned back around. He still had the knife.

"Billy," I said.

His eyes were reduced to quarter moons.

"Billy, come back here and sit down. Finish your story."

He turned the knife over, back and forth, in his palm. I could see Big Tex from the corner of my eye move his arm slowly toward Billy from behind, just in case. He shuffled toward us, but remained standing.

"Pretty soon I got this urge," he said. He moved his jaw around in a circle with his mouth open, as though it was hurting. "It was so powerful I didn't know what I was going to do. I was staring at his pathetic, sickly face, and I wanted to. . . you know. . . be close to him. I've never felt that way about somebody, a guy I mean. I felt like the whole world was crumbling down on top of me, because I had this feeling that I didn't want to have. I couldn't help it." Billy, who had dropped his head hiding his face in his hair, looked up at us. "I didn't." he said. "I didn't do anything. But, I wanted to. As sick as it sounds, I wanted him in the worst way; the fact that he might be dead made me want him even more because I knew he had passed beyond the plastic wrap of life; he knew the truth, and I didn't. I never had such a powerful feeling. He made me think of things. I saw myself in him. I saw my mom and dad. I saw all the girls I went through. I saw my soul being stuffed into a meat grinder, and out the other end fell greasy, muddy tears. I wanted to wake the guy up—I wanted to tell him!"

Suddenly, Billy twisted around and flung the fillet knife as far as he could into the darkness. Nobody said anything about what Billy said that night. His story was treated as some strange mistake, and it was never brought up again.

BUS RIDE THROUGH CLOUDS

With each new day and its clouds passing by overhead, I feel the helplessness of it all, and it makes me wonder where we're heading. Is everybody blind? Don't they see it? I see it. If you see it, you end up where I've ended up. I don't get it. I'm not lazy. I'm not without ambition. If I were, I wouldn't be sitting here riding on this bus. There's no place for people like us anymore, except in fields and factories. Pretty soon we'll be useless there too. I want to cry. I don't cry, I drink. I work. I fish. I do all that instead of crying. I don't think you understand me—I really do watch the clouds, every day, the way some people follow the news, or stock market. Everything you can imagine emerges from the clouds. Oh, I know, there's nothing permanent in them—they're gone as quick as they come. But that's why they fascinate me. They're the visual manifestations of moments, ideas, and thoughts. I watch the stars too, but the stars are harder to lose yourself in. It's easier to see change in the clouds, and it's the change that I'm really after. I am a cloud, not as pure, not as sure of myself, but as helpless, and, in some way that I now can't understand or admit or allow myself to fully believe, beautiful.

The bus was full of sweating, flat-tire bodies. I was wearing my suit. I unbuttoned the collar and loosened my tie as soon as the job fair was over. I kept wiping the sweat off my cheeks and forehead, and pushing it back into my hair. People were fanning themselves with newspapers and magazines. They were staring at me.

I was the only white guy on the bus, and the only guy in a suit. Of course, I knew why they were staring, and what they were thinking. I wanted to tell them who I was. They didn't know who I was. They saw my whiteness, they saw the suit, and recognized me. But they were wrong.

Mostly I looked out the window. When my eyes were focused in the bus, I made sure to stare and not look at anyone directly. I looked at the backs of heads. I saw one woman who had her hair cut short in back. She was a big woman. She had a double neck in back from all the fat there. It made me unconsciously move my own head. The line of her silhouette was like a sand dune so that you couldn't tell where her arm ended and shoulder began, or where her shoulder ended and neck began. She wore a pretty, bright dress. The straps of her bra showed plainly beside the straps of her dress and looked like sturdy basket handles. I felt like sleeping. I closed my eyes, but opened them for fear of something I could not identify. My feet hurt. The job fair was a waste of time. I'm not very good at first impressions. I don't like smiling when I'm not happy. I don't want to be one of *them*; it's just that I wouldn't mind having a little more money. It's time for somebody else to carry the load for a while. It was really pitiful. All those suits and ties, business cards, and phoniness; bullshit so well oiled it slipped from mouths like fucking diarrhea. Ten thousand fucking pharaohs telling me about the new world order. Not one of those assholes could give me an original thought, or think his way out of real trouble if he had his retirement portfolio hanging in the balance. What a waste of flesh. I felt eyes flashing all around me. One younger guy who sat in one of the side-facing seats stared openly at me, his arms dropped between his legs rolling a basketball on the floor between his feet. I wanted to turn to him and tell him to fuck off. Yeah, aggression is going to solve your problems. Here I am, the easy target. I'm the reason for all your shit. Whitey in suit and tie. Why do you think I'm on this fucking bus, asshole? You think this is *your* bus? You don't own this bus. You're a passenger just like me. You have no say in anything, and neither do I.

"You want to look at the Sports?" somebody said. It was the man sitting beside me across the aisle. He held out the rolled up Sports page. He'd taken it from the floor ten minutes earlier. "You want to see it?" he offered again. He smiled. In the five hours at the job fair I hadn't seen one single genuine smile. This man's smile, his entire presentation of the dirty rolled up Sports page, made me ashamed of my own anger. I took the paper from him.

"Anything good?" I asked him as I unrolled it.

"Baseball."

"Yeah? Who do you like?"

"I'm a Yankees fan, myself. Baltimore sometimes. In the National League I like St. Louis. The Yanks have won three in a row."

"Yeah, unfortunately for me. I'm a Tribe fan."

"Oh," the man said rolling back his eyes. "Well, at least we're not in the same division."

"Lucky for us. You guys always beat us."

"But you've had your fair share too. Everybody's got their nemesis."

"You guys are in a real dog fight this year. Boston's going to be hard to beat."

"Even harder in the post-season, if they get there. That's why we got to beat them in the division. I don't think a wildcard's going to come out of the East; so if we can beat them in the division, we won't have to face them. Man, Pedro himself can beat you in the post-season. Now that they've got your Manny, they're kind of scary."

"God, Manny," I said. "No offense, but at least he's not in pinstripes. I couldn't take that."

"Hey," the guy said. "You get on the wrong bus?"

"What do you mean?"

"You look like you should be driving some Mercedes, man! Look at you all dressed up in a suit and tie. I figured you must have got yourself on the wrong bus, or your Mercedes broke down."

I laughed out loud. "Me? You have the wrong guy."

"Where you going?"

"I've been there already. I was at a job fair."

"Job fair? What kind of job fair?"

"You know, the kind where everybody seems to want to meet you, but nobody needs you."

"Man," the guy said, his demeanor shifting some; he seemed almost mad. "You shouldn't be riding this *bus*. You need to get yourself a Mercedes. A guy like you shouldn't be riding this bus."

I shrugged my shoulders. "Only have one car, and the wife's working today."

"One car?" the man said incredulously, leaning back in his seat, looking at me from the corner of his eyes. "Aw, man. You need *two* cars. That's what you need."

I looked right at him, grinning. "I work at a nursery. I make five twenty-five an hour. Understand?"

"Five twenty-five an hour? You can make more at McDonald's flipping burgers," he said. "You need to get yourself a job where you're making some real money. You don't need to be working at no nursery."

"Thanks for the advice," I said. "I'm trying."

"Yeah. You need to get yourself something better," he said and

Ballad of the Confessor

turned to look straight ahead at all the bobbing heads.

I looked out the bus. I saw derelict buildings and weedy lots. I saw pawn shops, bars, corner markets, abandoned cars, broken concrete, peeling billboards, roiling games of basketball, beaten souls shuffling along and unbeaten, courageous souls with their heads held high. I felt my eyes tearing.

I blocked out the visions passing before me, but I found it impossible to close my eyes. I thought of Colorado. But the thought of Colorado wasn't big enough, and I began to think of Alaska. Alaska was different from Colorado. You don't need to be a cowboy there. I wouldn't be at such a disadvantage. It's more of a place to escape. That's what I wanted to do. I don't fit in. Even worse, I may be dangerous. I don't want to hurt anybody. But, I'm tired of being squashed by both sides. They both reject who I am, and I find nothing in either extreme that doesn't make me feel like using a machine gun on the whole damn lot. Left, right, up, down, blah-blah-blah-blah, lies and lies and lies. You have to choose sides. You have to choose sides on this bus, and back at the job fair, and at the nursery, and at home. I don't want to choose sides. I'm not on anybody's side. Nobody's on *my* side. They all want to grind you up so they can use you as powder for their agenda-canons. Well, they can shove that. I just want to go to Alaska and forget about this mess. I'm nothing here. I could croak tomorrow and nobody, including her, would notice. I'm a mule, a conveyor belt, a nail. The hyenas have won. There's nothing to do about it. Floods won't do it. Bombs won't do it. Building more jails won't do it.

The bus stopped, and more people got on. Some got off. I watched them out the window as the bus lurched forward. There was a man about my age with a woman, a girl about ten, and a baby. The man and woman passed the baby back and forth jabbering at each other while the girl played hopscotch on the sidewalk, and then began to dance without music, her braided hair flying up and down against her shoulders like strung candy. The man suddenly lifted the baby, smiling, and threw him gently into the air. The woman began walking down the sidewalk pulling at the back of her shorts. The girl, without looking up, followed, returning to the hopscotch, and then the man put his baby on his shoulders holding onto his tiny, puffy arms and followed his daughter. They don't know what they have. They think they know, but they don't. They're trying to bust out, like I'm trying to bust out. We're trying to bust out of different cages, and neither of us believes the other's is as real, or confining. This bus has just dropped off a lucky man. Someone who has nothing, and everything, trying to bust out. As long as he doesn't cannibalize himself, he'll be a happy man. But he'll never know, really, what he has. He'll only focus on what he wants.

I became sleepy, and closed my eyes. The lurching of the bus and its muffled whine nearly put me out. I dreamed something pleasant, I can't remember what it was. I awoke to the smell of french fries. The smell made me remember my hunger. I looked outside at the broken asphalt and weedy sumacs wedged between derelict buildings. A baby wailed toward the front of the bus. Two kids were being loud. One was asking for a piece of taffy, and the other was toying with him making him beg. I remembered my failure at the job fair. I became angry. I stared at the lolling heads and wanted to crush them all. I wanted to say something that would piss everybody off and create a riot. I thought about Mrs. John Carpenter and her white dress rippling in the wind. I let go, and imagined her standing in front of me by the picnic table, one hand touching my knee, the other hand lifting a fork of rhubarb pie to my mouth, the sparkle in her eye, knowing, heavy, unguarded. I imagined the feel of her fingers on my knee, then the contact of her leg as she pressed closer to feed me the pie; the tightness of her dress, the scent of her clean, rose petal neck. Then, she was strapped to the top of the picnic table, her arms secured with her own stockings as I pressed myself against her. Her smooth neck seemed to go on forever as I slid my nose and mouth up and down it, feeling the fullness of her body still encased by the dress. She whispered, urging me on. I cut her dress open and lay each half aside, exposing her white underpants and bra. Her chest heaved, her belly trembled. I talked dirty into her ear, causing her to smile and whisper back in her husky, little girl voice, "Please Mr. Wolf, don't do *tha'*. I a goo' little girl. I a goo', goo' little girl." For the next ten minutes I thought about one precise moment when I yanked down the front of her bra, pulled aside her white underpants and thrust into her, prompting a little girl gasp-squeak and her eyes to bug out. I thought of the moment over and over. I thought about it until it became unrecognizable, meaningless. When I decided to think of something else I was ashamed of myself, but any residual guilt soon disappeared and I was left feeling better about the bus ride and my failure at the job fair.

"Hey, man," I said to the new guy sitting next to me. "We getting close to the Cooper River Bridge?"

"The Cooper River Bridge?"

"Yeah. We getting close?"

"Sure. We're getting close. Not too far. Three, maybe four stops."

"There a bus that can take me over to Mt. Pleasant when I get off?"

"Mt. Pleasant? Yeah. Yeah, there's a bus that'll take you to Mt. Pleasant if you want. That where you want to go?"

I nodded.

"There's a bus maybe every half hour going across the river," the man said. He turned his head to look down at my clothes; his forehead wrinkled. "Man. You lost, ain't you?"

"Not really," I said.

"Your car break down?"

"No," I said. "I'm a bus inspector. Let me ask you; how do you find the service on this bus? Ever have any problems?"

"Problems? No, man. Gets kind of stuffy in here sometimes. Could use some air conditioning, you know. Maybe could be cleaned a little more often. But it ain't bad."

"Good," I said. "How about the driver? Any complaints there?"

"Aw, no," he said. "Melinda's a real good driver. She don't take no shit from her passengers. She's real good. The old people especially like her."

"You'd be willing to vouch for her, if there was ever an investigation?"

"You're not thinking of axing *her*, are you?"

"It's not up to me," I said. "I think she's safe. It's more the bus we're looking at."

The man turned to look straight ahead. His eyes were wide, he bit at his lip. When my stop came he let me know by nudging his sharp elbow into my side. He got up and stepped aside giving me a wide berth. I nodded, said so long, then turned to leave. He patted me on the back.

"Take it easy," he said.

I waited at the bus stop for five minutes, then began walking toward downtown. It was the middle of the afternoon. There was no reason to go home right away. I always feel like I have to be home, I don't know why. When I'm not home, I think I should be there. When I'm there, I think of being somewhere else. I stopped in a hamburger joint and ordered a plate of fries and a Coke. The place had a tall, coffered ceiling. Flies were everywhere. The flies hovered around my plate. I stared out the window, and at the counter girl who had long, brown legs. I watched her as she waited on the other customers. I paid close attention to her ears, hands, and waist. She caught me looking. I rattled my glass full of chopped ice and then took some in my mouth and chewed it, grinding it with my idling, overheating teeth. She reminded me of ten years earlier. The memory hurt to think about. I saw her look in the mirror behind the counter at me; flashing whites of eyes, and pink cheeks, and active lips blowing her bangs. I went up to the counter to pay. I didn't want to leave her.

"How was everything?" she asked in a perfunctory, chewing-gum cheerfulness. From the corner of my eye I noticed her checkered blouse expanding and contracting as she breathed.

"Good," I said.

She broke into a smile. "You got ketchup on your shirt."

I looked down. "Shoot."

"Two eighty-five," she said.

"Two eighty-five? Okay."

I pulled out my wallet and gave her the only bill, a ten, that I had. She held out her hand in a small cup, like I was going to put water in it. I made sure our hands touched, and when they did she glanced up; for the briefest moment she held her hand there, allowing it to linger against mine.

"You got a rag back there?" I asked her.

"Hold on," she said. She gave me my change. "Come around here," she motioned me over. She met me at the side of the counter. "Bring it closer," she said. I leaned toward her pushing out my chest. She pinched the wet rag so it had a small round end, then rolled it into the spot of ketchup. The feel of her hands through my shirt sent me into a panic. I looked at her brown face and pink lips and crystalline eyes. She was an ordinary-looking girl really; but to me, then, she was beautiful beyond words. "That's a nice suit," she said.

"Thanks." The suit was as cheap as they come.

"You just getting off work?"

"No," I said. I wanted to say more, but was frozen.

"So you're married," she said, glancing at my ring, then back up.

"Yup."

"Hmm," she said.

"Why?"

"Just wondering."

"You look like somebody," I said.

"I do? Who do I look like?"

"I'm not sure," I said. She moved the balled portion of the rag in little circles around the pink spot. Her earrings tinkled and her body bobbed sideways. "You work here a lot?"

"Every day, except Sundays and Tuesdays."

"Oh yeah? What do you do Sundays and Tuesdays?"

She lifted her eyes from my shirt. Her hand stopped moving. I thought my heart would explode. She smiled. "I go to the beach."

"The beach?"

"There," she said. She was finished, and leaned away from me. But she remained pushed into the counter looking at me with big, questioning eyes.

"Okay, thanks."

"Not a problem. You have a nice day then."

"I will," I said. "You do the same."

"Thanks," she smiled again.

"Thanks for the fries and Coke."

"Hey."

"What?"

"Nothing."

"What is it?"

"Nothing," she said again.

As I was sliding the change into my wallet, I watched her walk down the counter. She looked back at me twice.

Ballad of the Confessor

"So long," I said waving to her as I walked past the counter toward the door.

"Bye," she said.

"Good luck."

She grinned wryly. "With what?"

"I don't know," I shrugged. "Maybe I'll see you at the beach."

Everyone in the place heard me, but I didn't care.

THE BEACHED TURTLE

I lay awake on my back, fixated on the counter girl rubbing the wet rag against my shirt. I remembered everything about her. Her voice. Her look. Her smell. But most of all it was her touch. I'd forgotten what gentleness felt like. I was a stranger, yet she used her hands as though I were someone valuable, and worthy of affection. I wondered what I had done to earn her sweet benevolence. My heart quickened. I lay awake for most of the night unable to sleep.

My wife stirred; she let out a sigh. More than once I'd thought about killing her. I'd thought about it in a rage, and I'd thought about it soberly, methodically, the way you might plan a trip. I thought about the logistics, risks, and justifications. Whenever I weakened and pitied her, I'd remember all the times she came at me with fists, kicking, gouging, digging her nails into my flesh not for a warning, but in an attempt to do real damage. I remembered pushing her away, and her relentless pursuit of me. More than anything, I remembered what came out of her mouth. As grotesque as her physical assaults were, they paled when compared to the verbal barrages she threw at me, sometimes for hours at a time. Even in my room with the door closed she could reach me, and I felt her vi-

Ballad of the Confessor

ciousness. She knew where it hurt most, and there she dug the deepest. She clawed at the parts of me most vulnerable, where I was a child, where I was impotent, where I was afraid. She hid behind the protection of her sex, and her law. I fought back. I became practiced in the art of verbal retaliation, and then abuse. We went at each other like dogs. At times I couldn't take it. She'd grown up with it, but I hadn't. The words went deeper for me. The damage was not merely to the relationship, but to my self-worth. I had become frail, timid, paralyzed so that I could not leave. She'd seized control of me. She had destroyed my self-esteem to such a degree, that I knew I could not live on my own.

I thought about killing myself. The misery was too great. I had become one of *those* people, and that thought sickened me. As much as I hated her when she was attacking me, I pitied her, and despised myself for hurting her back. I tried it once. I bought some pills. I lay on the couch one day while she was out, took half the bottle, and thought about the end to the pain. I waited. My mind began to jerk about. My heart raced. Gradually, I went to sleep.

When I awoke she was home. I heard the sound of dishes being clinked together. There was a ringing in my ears. I knew I hadn't died. I hadn't even gotten sick. My eyes meandered around the ceiling. I heard the sound of slamming cupboard doors, and then, a while later, she came into the room and laid into me.

"You going to lie there all day? You're worthless. Get up, you lazy, fat, bald asshole. I know you can hear me. I said, get up. . . Do what you want, then. I'm going to the beach. I hate you. You're just an asshole. You're worthless."

It was only natural that over time my thoughts turned away from killing myself, to killing her. When I began to think more about it, it made more and more sense. *I* wasn't the one pummeling my self-esteem, making me miserable not wanting to come home. She was.

144

Yet, perversely, whenever I threatened to leave her she somehow reeled me back in, not by apologizing, but by pulling just the right strings. She made me believe it was all a game, that it was a calculated ploy on her part to make me see my own inadequacies. It worked. This cycle repeated itself often. After each episode I felt worse about myself, and was paralyzed by her threats to leave me. There was no alternative, but to kill her. Any other animal would do it. The government does it all the time, to people less deserving than her. They do it to mentally retarded people, for Christ's sake. Here was someone who consciously, systematically worked very hard at making me powerless, and miserable. She had turned me into a child, one foot from the loony bin. Isn't that a crime? I came to the conclusion that killing her might be the thing to do. But two things gave me pause: The first, and most obvious, was that murder is illegal. Having no experience in the murder department, I knew it was highly probable that I'd be caught. I thought about how I could do it and get away with it. My best solution, although far from foolproof, was to push her off a cliff while we were hiking. There were two such cliffs on our usual hike. A fall from either one would probably do the trick. If she didn't die, she'd at least be paralyzed. I didn't want that. Then I'd be saddled with her crippled, self-pitying soul for the rest of my life. The second reason for my hesitation was tied to the complex nature of her control over me: I understood where her abusiveness came from. She inherited it from her mom and dad. She was as innocent as I was. She never asked for it; I could no more blame her than I could someone born into poverty. Yet, she denied she was abusive. This denial was the gap in the bridge between us. Instead of trying to understand where it came from, she wouldn't accept that it was part of who she was. She was untreatable. I saw this, but I myself was in denial about the ship that was already sunk.

She moved again, sighing grumpily, as though I was taking up too much room on the bed. I felt like a burden. It was hot. She'd cast the sheets aside. I turned my head and looked at her body and was aroused, but then turned back to stare at the ceiling and think of the girl rubbing ketchup from my shirt.

When Sunday came I took my fishing gear and went over to Sullivan's Island. Twice during the week I went to the pay phone across the highway to call her, but both times I chickened out. As much as I wanted to see her, I couldn't escape the fact that I was still married. I came up with a real bright idea. I'd go to Sullivan's Island, maybe head on down to the Isle of Palms, and if I happened to bump into her, it'd be blind luck. I'd have done nothing wrong.

The hot wind hit me as I walked through the scrubby sea bushes, and I heard the sound of the waves gushing gently up into the sand. There was nobody in my usual spot. I put two lines out, then sat down on my cooler and poured a beer between my legs into a plastic cup. I shoved the empty bottle into the ice beneath the two paper bags of shrimp, then looked to the water where it was dark near the horizon for the black submarines. The sky seemed bleached by the bright sun, and the clouds faded into the slate blue like strands of cotton candy. The water was calm. There was hardly any surf at all. Only at the very end would a wave turn over on itself in a polite, high-pitched tumble. I caught two small blues, but threw them back. I squatted in the water and washed off my hands, then wiped them on my shorts. I looked down the beach. She was probably at the Isle of Palms. That's where you'd go if you were young and wanted to be in a crowd. That's why I never go there except with Lonnie. You can't fish there. My main thing is fishing. Looking at oiled bodies is only incidental to the fishing. I sat back down. I wore my straw hat. I bought the hat at a Reggae festival last year for five bucks; the edges were frayed and made interesting shadows in the sand when I dipped my head and moved it sideways. I wondered what kind of bikini she wore. She wasn't very dark for going to the beach every Sunday and Tuesday. Maybe she didn't swim, or sunbathe, but walked beaches looking for shells, or sea life. Maybe she was interested in ecology. Or maybe she brought an umbrella with her and read books. I wondered what kinds of books somebody who works at a hamburger joint reads. I wondered what she was doing with herself. Maybe she was in college. I thought about her standing in the water in her bikini. In my fantasy the sun was going down, the sky was pink, her body glowed as she slowly entered the gentle wakes. I could barely look at her because of her beauty. She swam out near the buoy. I could only see the round shimmering of her head as she pushed toward the buoy. I met her there. We hung onto the sides floating on our stomachs, our legs out as though we were flying. She was a marine biology major. She said she went scuba diving once a month, and that I should go with her sometime, she could teach me. We pushed off the buoy and took our time swimming to shore. We swam on our backs, the blazing sun smacking our faces. We lay down on our towels on our stomachs. She combed her hair in rough strokes. I put on my straw hat looking straight ahead at some washed-up, bleached pieces of lumber, my chest still heaving from the swim.

"What do you do?" she asked me.

"I work at a nursery," I told her.

"Oh," she said with surprise. "You like plants. You're like me." She smiled.

"I guess so," I said. "It's just what I do. I can't say I'm there by choice."

"Then why are you there?" The water was beginning to dry on her skin, but new drops were being flicked on her arms and back from her combing.

I didn't know the real answer to her question, so I gave her the short answer. "Because I'm not somewhere else."

She thought my answer was funny. "You must like it, or you wouldn't be there."

"How old are you?"

"Twenty-one."

"Well, you're working at Jacque's, aren't you? Are you there because you want to be there?"

"Yeah," she said with real conviction. "It's getting me through school."

"And the nursery's getting me through something too; it's just not as well-defined as school."

"You should be a marine biologist," she said, her eyes lingering on me. "You'd be good at it."

"What makes you think so?"

"I can tell," she said.

"Actually, you're right. I always wanted to be a marine biologist. I'm a strong swimmer." I held up my arm and made a muscle. She felt it. It was the second time her hand, her actual skin, touched mine. The first time had been at the diner when I gave her the ten.

"You don't have to be strong to be a marine biologist," she said.

"You don't."

"No. You just have to love things."

At that precise moment, I fell in love with her. I decided to enroll at the College of Charleston to get a degree in marine biology. I didn't have the money. I'd have to borrow it, or get it from somewhere. I'd move out, right off. I didn't care where I lived. I didn't care about anything but getting the degree and being with her.

I came out of the fantasy feeling good. I checked the lines. One hook was stripped, and the other had only bits and pieces hanging from it. I took the booger-glob and tossed it in the sand and watched as a speckled-egg colored gull came flap-running over and snatched it up. He waited for more, along with some others who had seen him feeding. I baited my lines, waded out to my thighs, then hurled them out as far as I could. I set the rods in their holders and pulled the lines taut. I had plenty of shrimp. I took one bag and sat down on the cooler and fed the gulls, breaking the shrimp in half. I wanted them to catch the shrimp in mid-air. There was one noisy, bully gull. I avoided him as best I could, instead aiming at the smaller, more timid ones. I attracted the attention of two crows, and a few sandpipers. Both the crows and sandpipers stayed on the fringes of the crowd, and neither got any of the shrimp.

"That's all," I said. I waved the empty bag at them. "No more."

I checked the tension on the lines, then started down the beach. There were some cargo ships off near the horizon, so faded you had to look for them against the hazy blue-gray of the afternoon. I saw a group of people up ahead. They looked like they were circled around a big heap of garbage bags. As I drew closer, I realized they weren't garbage bags. I couldn't tell what they were until I was almost upon them. It was a beached sea turtle. The poor bastard must have weighed three hundred pounds, and lay four feet high. Its head was the size of a square watermelon. The whole thing was dark from the early process of decay. It oozed in spots, which attracted excited clans of biting flies. There was shock and bewilderment on the faces of the people gathered around, but some beach strollers only slowed down to look without stopping, the way people slow to look at accidents.

"What kind is it?" some pony-tailed girl asked this guy. She was too young to be fantasizing about, but because the back of her wedgy-bathing suit was giving me a clear shot at her left adolescent onion-ass cheek, I couldn't help myself. The guy seemed to be the self-appointed dead sea turtle guru. The girl gave off a complex expression of sadness and nausea.

Ballad of the Confessor

"We think it's a loggerhead," the man said.

"Who's *we?*" I asked him, but nobody listened.

"What happened to it?" the girl sniffled.

"Well," the man said with a long sigh, as though he'd told the story many times already, "it's hard to say. It might have gotten tied up in some fishing lines, though we don't see any cuts on it. It might have a disease. Or, it could have died from old age," he said.

The girl pushed out her lower lip. "It's so sad," she said.

"Did anybody call the police?" some lumpy middle-aged woman in a one-piece Speedo asked. She was one of those who couldn't help herself, and poked the turtle in places where it was oozing.

"They've been out already," the man said. "They'll be back later with chains to haul it off."

"What will they do with it?" the girl asked.

"I don't know," the man, who reminded me of my old high school counselor, even though my old counselor was a woman, said. "I'm sure they'll want to find out why it died."

"It's just so sad," the girl whimpered.

The man placed his hand on her arm. "It was probably time," he said to her; he kept stroking the arm that was connected to the body I was currently flying through the sky-orgy with. "They'll probably find that he lived a good, long life. There's every reason to believe it."

"Why don't we eat it?" I said. All the sad faces turned toward me; I felt like Caesar just before he got hacked. The woman in the Speedo nodded her head eagerly. "Well, it's *dead*," I said in my own defense.

I couldn't help myself and I began to laugh. Everything about the scene struck me as being ridiculous.

"Guess some people think the death of an endangered animal is funny," I heard the man say as I was walking away. I knew he was talking directly to the wounded girl. That's how things like that work.

When I got back to my poles I checked the lines. They were both stripped clean. I re-baited and cast them back out, then lay down on my towel and sipped another beer. One line went down. I jumped up, took the pole in my hands and jerked it back, reeling as fast as I could. I felt the fish tug the line in quick succession, and as I reeled I felt the heaviness and knew it was a good one. I walked toward the water, reeling, keeping the pole high. As I brought it closer to shore it felt more heavy than powerful. I reeled in steady, easy strokes. It was a flounder, good-sized. I let it down away from the water on the wet sand. His speckled back was smooth to the touch, his two eyes stared helplessly up at me. I flipped him over to see the beautiful white bottom. He was hooked pretty good, so I dipped him in the water to wash off the sand, removed the hook from his mouth and put him in the cooler on top of the shrimp and ice and beer. I re-baited, then cast back out. I sat down on the cooler wiping my hands off on my shorts. It was nearly five o'clock. I realized she wasn't going to come. I hadn't really expected to see her, yet I was deflated. I should have called her and told her to meet me. Why didn't I? She'd have come. The day would have been wonderful. We could be swimming out there right now. I'd be squirting water at her through my teeth. I'd tickle her. The tickling would turn serious. We'd be kissing. Something caught my eye. I looked up. It was a submarine. It was going up towards the river. I watched until it disappeared. I checked the slack in the lines, then went in for a swim. I waded in up to my knees, then made my arms into a spear point and dived in. I swam beneath the water, coming up for air, then going back down. I twisted myself like a corkscrew upside-down blowing the air out my nose, then floated on my back and thought about having to get back home. Lonnie had dropped me off, but I'd have to hitch a ride or hoof it the whole way. The day flew by. Where'd it go? I didn't want

Ballad of the Confessor

to think about work, but I did. I hate Sundays, really.

I reeled in my lines and packed up. I let the water out of the cooler and dumped some of the ice to lighten the load. I started walking. I passed through the dune hedges onto the open grass at the fort ruins. There's an eloquence there on that open space of grass with the ramparts and earthworks and huge cannons waiting for time to round their sharp edges down to nothing. There's a scent of youthful, animal brutality that I find soothing.

BRIDGE OF FEARS

Eddie's what they call a deadbeat dad. He doesn't pay his child support. Most of the girls at the nursery don't like him, all because he's a deadbeat dad. Roxy still likes him, but she's the only one. Even Evelyn, who finds good things to say about everybody, doesn't go for Eddie too much. Eddie doesn't defend himself. He's too busy working. He's got three kids with his current wife, and two kids from an ex-wife. His ex-wife was pregnant when they got divorced; the child wasn't Eddie's. She married the father of the child, a guy who conveniently had money. His income doesn't count when child support is calculated. The less she works, the more Eddie has to work. The girls gossip about Eddie nearly every time he walks by, if only in the frowns and mean faces they make. People need things to hate. When there's a shortage of things to hate, somebody somewhere creates them. Eddie absorbs the hate from the girls so they don't have to lay it on their husbands and boyfriends; it gives the ones who know they'll never get a man reason to pity themselves, and lay the blame where it doesn't belong. Eddie, he's a hatred sponge. I don't know where he wrings out the hatred he's drenched in. I think it'd probably eat me up.

Ballad of the Confessor

We have three horticultural specialists at the nursery—three girls all in their late twenties. I don't know their names. I do, but I don't care. They're all different, but they're all the same. When they get together they start yick-yacking about Eddie, or sometimes me or Reggie because we don't move too fast. Nobody who's ever worked one single day moving trees when it's one hundred degrees and ninety-five percent humidity has ever made the comment, "That guy's moving too slow." I like everything about Eddie, even if he is a deadbeat dad. Everybody has their ugly parts. Why do they all have to use him as their personal whipping boy? Why are women always bitching about things? Why don't they just shut the hell up and do their God damn job? I don't know; maybe it's the times. But I'll tell you what; it makes me want to puke, all the crap I hear around here about this guy and his problems, or that guy and his problems. Do women ever stop to think that maybe we don't give a rat's turd if the living room's fancy shmancy enough to be featured on Martha Stewart? No, they don't. They only bitch about how we don't help them with their obsessions. Bitch, bitch, bitch. Man, I've had a lifetime of it.

I was sitting in the sun one afternoon resting. I wasn't on official break. I was just sitting near the three Medusas listening to them squawk; I thought I'd show them how a real workingman could sit down any old time he liked and rest his weary body. I wanted them to look at me. I wanted to stare back when they did. *Come on, say something,* I thought. Say something and watch ten years of being bitched at explode like a volcano.

Me and Reggie went fishing out on Sullivan's Island after work. It was the first time I went fishing during the week in a long time. Somebody was in our spot, so we moved down a few hundred feet. There were more dunes alive with blowing sea oats in the new spot. The tide was up. There was only a thin strip of sand that stayed dry.

We had a great breeze because we were exactly on the point where the island bends away from the open sea. The breeze was cool; the water was choppy and green-gray. We were using shrimp, and cut mullet, getting some hits but they weren't staying on.

"Probably crabs," I said.

"Most likely," Reggie said. His eyes looked far out to the horizon. I don't know what he was looking at, or for. The horizon's a chameleon of temptations, and a living, breathing truth serum. It's a way to speak to God in a simple language. For me, it's the only way. Whenever I see men sitting on buckets fishing looking out over the broad sea, I know they're conversing with God. I don't believe in the garden story. I believe we came from the sea, just like frogs and turtles. I don't see what's wrong with that. I don't believe in the original sin theory either. I believe we came from the sea long ago on our bellies, and now we walk upright like birds only without wings. Why does there have to be a garden story, or an original sin theory to cloud people's lives? People who believe those things make me suspicious. I quit going to church years ago. I got tired of being yelled at. I already felt bad about myself; I didn't need some priest heaping it on even more. My wife, she says she wants to go to church. But she never does. She says it's because I won't go with her. She says she'd be too embarrassed to be seen without me. I don't think she believes in things the way I believe in things, or the way Reggie does. I think she's like most people, and wants to do the proper thing. She thinks going to church is one of those proper things. Well, that's kind of juvenile if you ask me. I guess people like you more if you do things the proper way, even if what you're doing is ridiculous. People like you less if you actually use your brain and think for yourself; that ranks high up on the intimidation scale. Think of all the brainpower we have. As an adult, you're supposed to suppress it. You're supposed to use your brain to maintain proper, acceptable forms of behavior. We're like those worms me and Reggie catch, except they get to use every ounce of feeble brainpower they have tunneling through the ground. The more brains you have, the less you're supposed to use them.

About two years ago I decided to do something; I didn't want to go crazy listening to the wind howl through my empty skull, so I decided I'd allow myself to think whatever I wanted, as long as I still acted the way I was expected to. It didn't take long before I started having problems. The more I allowed myself the freedom to think, the closer I got to going crazy. I thought the freedom would cure me, when all it did was emphasize my bondage. It was twice as bad as before. I tried to stop thinking so much, but I had trouble turning it off now that I'd got it going. It's like it had a will all its own apart from me; it fought like an animal to stay alive! I was in a real bad way. I had to do something—my freewheeling mind was going to eat through my phony exoskeleton, and my real self was going to spring out onto the world and get me shot on sight. That's when I invented the game. Since I couldn't stop my mind any more than I could stop a train, I thought I could at least determine, to some degree, where it went. I decided that every time my mind was getting ready to bust out, I'd have it work on my imaginary bridge. I was building a bridge from the earth to the moon. There was somebody on the moon who was starting there working toward me. She was just like me, alone, going crazy from not being able to think what she wanted. The problems with constructing such a project were monumental. The biggest challenge was how to make sure our two bridges lined up with each other in outer space. We had no way to communicate, except that we both knew we were mirrors of each other; our struggles, our confinements, our regurgitation of thoughts, our desires—they were identical. In essence, we were working with our silent selves on the other end. The bridge was not an ordinary bridge. We weren't going to transport our bodies across it; we were going to transport our fears. If you think the bridge was going to be like some kind of telephone or computer line, then you're wrong. Telephone lines can't transport fears, and neither can computer cables. This new bridge would not transport representations of our fears, but would move the fears themselves—they would slip from our minds and cross somewhere out in space. The problem of figuring out how to construct such a bridge was one thing; but what would happen when our fears crossed and then landed in each other's lap, well, that was something else.

It was a few days later, I was waiting out front under the tree waiting for my ride. Everybody who was waiting for rides had been picked up; I was left alone, still waiting, the sun shining like an ice pick in my eyes. I realized my wife wasn't coming. She does that sometimes when she's mad. Once, I ran over to Skippy's Bar on the island from our apartment and she met me there for dinner. We had a fight and she stomped out of Skippy's and left me there to run back home in the dark, when she knew I barely made it there in the first place. She's like that. She doesn't care about anything else when she's mad. She thinks her anger takes priority over everything, and justifies me being hit by a truck, or stepping into a pothole and breaking my ankle.

I figured I better start walking. I got up, my feet were sore. I didn't know how I was going to make it. I was a mile down the road when this car swerved over into the grass ahead of me and stopped. I ran up to it and saw it was Barb. Barb is one of the three Medusas.

"You want a ride?" she said. Her car was an old, rusty Chevette.

"Sure," I said and got in the passenger side. I pulled the door shut three times before it finally latched.

"Lock it," she told me.

"Lock it?"

Ballad of the Confessor

"It'll pop open if you don't lock it."

I watched the rubber spider hanging from the rear view mirror swing back and forth. It was strange seeing it from the inside after seeing it all those times from the outside. Barb was a maniac driver. She drove with her hands up on the wheel like they teach you in driver's ed, her nose pushed forward like she was watching for a deer or a tractor. She never looked over at me once the entire time we were moving.

"You saved me from having some tired feet tomorrow," I said.

"You don't mind if we stop at my place first, do you?"

"Sure," I said. Nothing mattered to me now that my feet were saved. "You know where I live, don't you?"

"I bought some ice cream bars and they'll melt."

Barb and I used to be friends. I never used to lump her in with the other two Medusas when we were friends. She was about the only person I talked to for a while because there didn't seem to be anything I could say that really shocked her. In fact, what everybody else considered shocking made her laugh.

"So how's it been going?" I asked her.

"The witch leave you to walk home again?"

"Seems that way."

"Gee, isn't that a surprise."

Barb hated me these days. After we became friends, she fell in love with me. I never saw it coming. One day I opened up my paper bag lunch and there was a note in it. The note wasn't from my wife—it was from Barb. She told me how she couldn't stand it anymore, that she just had to tell me or she'd kill herself: She was head over heals in love with me. When I read the note I felt a gush of confusion and embarrassment. She stopped by later in the day after she knew I'd read it, and all I could do was laugh. I knew it was about the worst thing I could do under the circumstances, but I was

158

so unprepared for it that I laughed.

"No, you don't," I'd told her.

She gave me a look.

"Come on," I said. "You gotta be kidding. Me?"

I was so embarrassed I hid the note in my paper bag and threw it out at the end of lunch. I treated it like a hiccup. I thought we'd go on as friends the way we'd been. But of course, the exact opposite happened. From that day forward, she hated me. She ignored me, or made ridiculous, adolescent faces at me. As time went on, I understood why she hated me. I'd told her all about the way it was at home. She listened. I thought she was listening the way Reggie listened. But she was a lonely heart listening, imagining I was on the other end of the bridge we were building together. I told her often how I was going to leave my wife. I thought we had one thing, and she thought we had something else.

We pulled into her apartment, some low, pre-fab building that looked like a spaceship. She reached back for the bag of ice cream bars and whipped it from the car into the air like it was alive. I leaned my knee against the door after I got out and pushed on it until I heard it click.

"This is my lovely home," she said. A guy across the lawn was standing beside another spaceship building holding his small dog by a leash as it sniffed around his bare feet. He lifted a soda can at Barb. Barb rolled her eyes and said to me, "Hello, Scott, you psychotic Peeping Tom. Yes, this is my boyfriend. My *boyfriend*. Do you understand what a boyfriend is? Keep your telescope pointed away from my window or you'll find another dead furry animal on your windshield. *God*. Aren't you pathetic. . ."

Thistles flanked her doorstep on both sides. She unlocked the door, and we went in. Her apartment was like a cave. All the windows were covered up with Venetian blinds and dated, gold-colored

Ballad of the Confessor

curtains. It was small. The layout was in a square, with the kitchen on one side of the steps and the living room on the other side. The steps were the dominant feature to the first floor, and thrust up to the second floor like a huge dagger. The living room was tidy, loaded with books stacked high against the walls. On one of the shelves was a collection of spiders. She had all different kinds and all different sizes, but most of them were black. Candles sat in saucers around the floor. The place smelled like evergreen incense. I stood in the middle of the floor with my hands in my pockets feeling like maybe I shouldn't be looking at anything. She came out from behind the steps, and for the first time she looked right at me.

"Well, what do you think?" she asked me. I naturally couldn't tell her what I really thought, so I told her she had a nice place. She asked me if I wanted a beer, but I told her no thanks. "I'm going to get changed first," she said. "You don't mind, do you?" I lied and told her I didn't mind at all. She turned on some music and started making small talk. I didn't like the way things were going; she seemed to be stalling. There was a funny look in her eyes, and then she began moving her body to the music with her eyes dilated or closed completely, her hands floating in the air—like I wasn't even there. I tried to chop up the mood with ridiculous questions.

"Where'd you get this?" I asked her, picking up a tiny gnome that was sitting on the corner of her bookshelf.

"Come on," she said, pulling on my hands.

"Come on where? Where're we going? Hey—you smoke something over there?"

"Come on," she urged me again. For the first time there was a feminine softness to her voice. Warning lights flashed and sirens blared inside my head.

"I can't," I said, tugging my hands away and putting them back in my pockets.

"You're such a square," she laughed. Her hands rose high above her head; she wiggled like a belly dancer. I whistled and moved my head purposely out of step with the music. She lifted her work shirt from her khakis showing her stomach and the silvery belly ring there shining like a piece of shrapnel. She laughed at me again, and went to poke me in the stomach, but I swerved away and laughed asking her, "What are you doing?" She trudged upstairs to change.

I was tired, but I didn't sit down. I waited in the middle of the room kicking the brown carpet, then read the titles to the books on her shelves without them registering anything. I just kept reading keeping my brain occupied until I could escape. I hadn't heard any sounds for some time. I called up to her. She gave no reply. I waited, then called up again. I was thinking what a nut case she was, when she called down.

"You ready?"

"Ready," I said.

"No," she said, "are you *ready*?" I heard strange, hissy-crinkly noises like somebody was going through Easter basket straw.

She began descending the stairs. Everything collapsed into some otherworldly joke-dream once I saw her bare foot, and then the white hem of her dress. She came down in slow motion. My eyes felt stabbed. I wanted to rocket through the ceiling into the sky. She stood before me in a white wedding dress.

The brownness of her face and arms contrasted with the whiteness of the dress in terrifying beauty. She'd removed her thick glasses and looked at me cross-eyed, her lips parted to allow big, swooping breaths of nervousness to flow in and out of her lungs; the bodice of her dress throbbed like ocean surges.

"I bought it four years ago," she said. She sounded like someone else. She looked like someone else. In my confusion I found her irrepressibly attractive. "I thought we were going to be married," she

Ballad of the Confessor

said. "He told me we were. We were in love. I thought he finally was the one. I told everyone that we were getting married. I even picked out a date." Only her lips moved as she stood in a trance, remembering the event which had shattered her hopes, and would shape the rest of her life. "But he never asked me. I assumed that because we talked about it, he didn't need to actually ask me. We were going to elope down at Hilton Head. I had everything reserved. I drove down twice with my sister. It was going to be at sunrise near the jetty; I had the spot picked out. After all the others, after the religion, after the health clubs and bars, I thought I'd found him. I realized a week before the wedding that he wasn't going to marry me." She seemed to be deliberating over the memory, as though still after all this time she had not worked it out in her mind. "I don't think he's a bad person. He just didn't want to marry me. That doesn't make him a bad person, does it? I went down to Hilton Head anyway. I already had the hotel room reserved. I didn't think it would affect me. But how couldn't it? On Saturday I put on the dress and walked down to the spot on the beach. It was early. I passed fishermen who wished me good luck. Some told me that if the guy backed out they'd take his place. I stood on the spot until the sun was high. I stood there all day long. I still had hope that he'd change his mind. I wanted to punish myself for being so foolish, and for thinking I could have him. I was there on the same spot, sitting in the sand as night fell. No one approached me. They all walked around me like a hole in the sand." She turned toward me with her crossed eyes and shimmering neck. "So you see, I've never recovered. I thought I would. But now I know I never will. I've become defined by it; I've turned away from that moment, which passed me by, and am really only waiting for God to even things out."

THE SECRET

It's been over a hundred now for five days. I keep a bottle of salt water with me wherever I go. This morning Reggie and I moved trees. His shoulder is getting better, but he's still not a hundred percent. He doesn't milk the injury anymore. In fact, he pushes harder than he should. I tell him to take it easy, and he tells me, "Aw, boy, my shoulder's just fine." He walks with his old stiff sturdiness, even in this heat. He got a haircut, and the haircut because it's so short makes him look like somebody else, maybe a brother. It emphasizes the fleshiness of his cheeks and jaw and throws the whole balance of his head off. Less hair and more flesh makes him seem even more rugged. He reminds me of a buffalo. Before lunch the boss told us to spread fresh mulch under the roses. That meant we first had to move all the roses out. The boss was being considerate because of the heat. It was meant as an easy job.

"Where's your water?" I said to Reggie when we were having lunch. We were in the back of the nursery under the trees.

"Left it at the trailer."

"You're going to die without it."

"I'll get it."

Ballad of the Confessor

I had two bologna sandwiches for lunch. My stomach was dying for something. The bologna tasted like heaven, even though I don't like bologna. I looked over at Reggie's sandwich.

"Hey. What kind you got?"

"Meatloaf," he said with a lurch.

"Homemade meatloaf?"

"Uh-huh."

"Your wife make it?"

"Uh-huh."

"Bologna," I said, lifting my hand. Reggie nodded with disinterest. "With ketchup and mustard." I looked at Reggie's big zip-lock bag of potato chips enviously, though I don't too often eat potato chips on account of it's just like pouring sludge into your arteries. "Hey."

Reggie moved his eyes over.

"So, we're moving the roses?"

"You heard the boss."

"That's nothing. The afternoon oughtta fly."

Reggie made a noise and moved his eyes away again.

I couldn't keep from gulping water and before I finished my two sandwiches it was gone. I still had some cut pieces of broccoli and an apple. I kept telling myself the heat would pass. We were in the peak of it; it couldn't get much worse. I thought about fall with its cool, dry days.

"What happened to Lyle?" I asked him a while later.

"Moved on."

"He get canned, or he just move on?"

"Moved on."

"Back to the Merchant Marines?"

"Beats me," he said.

"I don't know."

"You don't know what?"

"I don't know about that Lyle."

Reggie didn't say anything. He ate a few potato chips picking them up one by one with the tips of his fingers, like they were some delicacy. "Kind a lazy," he said.

"We getting anybody else?"

"Sure. Boss always gets somebody else."

"When they starting?"

"Mm-*mm*-mm," Reggie shrugged. "Pretty soon, I guess."

A week ago Reggie's boy was stopped by police. He and some friends drove to USC in Columbia for some parties. They were heading out of town about two in the morning when a cop pulled them over. They told Reggie's son to get out of the car, and when he asked them what for they told him to shut up and just get out of the car. They made him walk a line, then close his eyes and touch his nose. They made him bend over the hood of the car with his arms and legs spread and they felt through his clothes for a weapon. The boy asked them why they stopped him and one cop said he fit the description of somebody they were looking for who robbed a convenient store. Ever since his friend got shot, he was clean as could be. He didn't smoke, drink, or hang out with trouble magnets. They told him to open up the trunk of the car. He told them he wouldn't do it. He told them they didn't have any right, that he didn't do anything wrong. He said he had friends in law school who told him what was what concerning searches and seizures, and there wasn't no way he was going to open his trunk for them or anybody else. They told him fine, get in the squad car, punk. The other kids drove home. Reggie had to drive to Columbia the next morning to pick him up. They charged the boy with resisting arrest, but then dropped it after the boy called his law school friends. For the last three days Reggie's gone fishing with his son. He's been on the quiet side, and doesn't seem to be listening when I say something.

About one o'clock the boss came over and told us the new guy was starting this afternoon. He said he was at the trailer now, and he'd be over in a few minutes. Ten minutes later this tall, soft-looking marshmallow character came strolling down the path with his head up in the air like he was watching birds. We stopped and watched the guy, who wandered on down toward the shade plants. About ten minutes later the guy came back through the path that cuts right in the middle of the roses. He stopped and looked at us shyly. He had long hair that covered his ears and brushed his eyebrows. His thumbs were stuck in the belt loops of his jeans.

"I' aneewo' he-a named Re-ee?"

Reggie looked at me, then back to the stranger. "What the hell did you say?" he said.

"I look-ee fo' Re-ee," the guy said.

"Reggie? You're looking for Reggie?" I asked him. He nodded with embarrassment. "Well," I lifted my arm and pointed, "there's your man right there."

He walked over to Reggie and lowered his head, his right foot kicking at the mulch. "My name i' To-ny," he said. "I wuk wi' you."

Reggie stood with his mouth open, staring up at the guy's head. Tony stood at least six-six.

"You're the new fella," Reggie said. "Damn, son. You're a tall one."

Tony moved his head around like he was testing out the hinge on his neck, still looking vaguely at the ground, embarrassed. Reggie gave me a look. I knew exactly what he meant by it. We found ourselves a real brute.

Tony didn't say another word the rest of the afternoon. He may have been soft looking, but he was stronger than anybody I'd ever worked with at the nursery, including Lyle. He pinched four three-gallon roses in each set of fingers, where me and Reggie only carried two. And he did it with an effortless embarrassment, as though he could do more but didn't want to make us look bad. Tony took orders well. He did exactly as Reggie told him. When we stopped for a break, he kept working. Reggie told him to cut it out—"Hey, man, you're gonna overheat if you don't rest some." But Tony kept moving. He sweated enough, but his breathing was smooth and easy, like it was nothing. I told him about the salt tablets and how he ought to get himself a bottle and fill it with salt water, and keep it with him wherever he went; at least until it cooled off some. Once all the roses were moved off, we had to get the mulch. Me and Tony sat on the back of the trailer with our legs dangling over the edge as Reggie drove the tractor to the mulch pile.

"Tony," Reggie said, "you get up there on the pile and toss it onto the trailer. I'll even it out. Now don't overdo it. Take it easy, son, there's no hurry."

Me and Tony climbed the mulch pile, which was a good twelve feet high. He was something to see. He stood in one place, thrust the pitchfork into the wall of mulch, swung his body and arms around like some human backhoe, then dumped it onto the trailer. He never stopped to rest. He never paused to see where he would dig next. When Reggie told him that was enough, he scrambled down from the pile, jumped up onto the trailer, and in huge effortless strokes began evening out the heap. Me and Reggie got out of his way. When we got to the roses Reggie told Tony to toss the mulch down while we spread it out. We couldn't keep up, and soon Tony was down helping us spread the mulch. He used his pitchfork because we had only two rakes.

"Here," Reggie said handing Tony his rake. "You wanna use this? We'll be back in a few minutes. You keep working. Take a break when you're tired. Don't want you dying on me."

Ballad of the Confessor

We went down to the trailer. Roxy was helping some customers. I waved. She waved. I dropped two salt tablets into my empty bottle. Reggie put three in his, which was still sitting where he left it. As we were filling up with water Mike, Mitch, and Boog walked up.

"What're you guys doin'?" Reggie asked them. None of them had tools. They were barely sweating.

"Us?" Mitch said with guilt splashed all over his face.

"You guys up to no good?"

"Not us," said Mike, cutting the air on *us*.

"Yeah, okay."

"Bowman give you guys the day off?" I asked them.

"Hell no," Mitch said. "Today's cleaning day."

"Cleaning day?"

"Bowman told us to clean out the trucks."

"That'll take you about an hour," Reggie said.

"Oh, *nooooooooo*. It took us what, Mike—two, two and a half? Now we're going to spray off all the tools. And then we're going to clean up this mess."

"What for?" Reggie said. "So you can mess it up again?"

"Bowman's orders," Mitch said. "Have to do what the man says." The five of us wandered around the trailer toward Roxy, who was now sitting alone beneath the shade of the awning.

I sidled up next to Mike. "Bowman really tell you it was cleaning day?" I asked him.

"Yes," he said. "He and Eddie went on a two man job in town. They'll be gone all day. He says we've been working hard. It's hot. Reall-lly, reall-lly hot. I think he's a good man for giving us such a break, don't you think?"

"Sure. A man can't work day in and day out when it's like this. It's liable to kill him. Mike, you just make sure those salt pills don't disappear."

"Yeah, and leave my ketchup sandwiches alone," Mitch, who had heard me, chimed in with mock seriousness.

"Turkey snatcher," Mike came back playfully.

Mitch suddenly twisted his head around. "Hey, Reg', I hear you got a new body in today."

Reggie gave no reply.

"I hear he's a real idiot. A real Dumbo," Mitch said.

"We got somebody," Reggie nodded. "His name's Tony."

"Tony? Might as well be Dumbo. Where'd they get that guy, anyway? From the retard factory? Bet they got him from the retard factory—right off the bus."

"Oh, he'll be just fine," Reggie said.

"Where is he? I wanna say hello to him."

"Hey Mitch," I said. "Just drop it."

"Drop what?"

"I don't want you messing with Tony," I said. I made sure he saw my seriousness. "You hear me?"

"Who said I was going to mess with him? I just wanna meet him."

"Yeah, well, you heard me. I gave you fair warning."

"Come here," Mike said pulling on my shirt. As the other three walked up to Roxy, we stood about fifteen feet out from the desk. "Just pretend that you're talking to me. Say anything—it doesn't matter. When you get a chance, look over. You can see right up Roxy's skirt."

"Okay. Settle down, Mike. Come on—she'll know what we're doing. You go to the zoo today? Hot dog. Hot dog."

"Yesterday I see fine. Oh, man. Reptilians."

"A big watermelon filled with peaches and. . . coconuts."

"Lord," Mike said, his voice cracking. "She's got *nothing* on. Peanut brittle. Oh, Lord. Peanuts. Peanuts. . ."

Ballad of the Confessor

"Ho-ly, would you believe. . ."

"Turkey sandwiches. Turkey sandwiches," Mike said in a flurry. Roxy, who was now engaged in conversation, glanced over every so often with what appeared to be either a knowing smirk, or a blank stare. With her you could never tell. "What makes a girl do something like that?" Mike stammered. "Turkey. Turkey. Turkey. What? She has to know."

"Shh," I told him. "Easy. You keep looking at me. I want another peek."

I turned ever so slightly toward her. My eyes moved like wildfire from the dirt in front of us up toward the awning. Beneath the shadow of the table Roxy's feet sat side-by-side, a foot apart. Her shoes had been kicked off. She wore a silver-colored nail polish that sparkled when she moved. Her toes flitted like little birds; her shins and knees were a smooth, pale hue, more naked-looking than tanned skin. She had begun to move her knees together, then apart, in a sort of accordion rhythm. Each time her legs opened it was like a ball of light appeared, and for a snap of the fingers there it was, there *she* was, in all her naked glory. Each flash was like a stroke of air being pumped into my weary soul, expanding my deflated hope, forcing the atrophied parts of my masculinity into action. Her white nakedness contained no moral dilemma—there was only her female allure, and my male readiness. My eyes traveled upward. Roxy was looking right at me. I locked my eyes on hers, waiting for her to break it. She didn't. Even as Mitch sat beside her on the desk with his hands practically massaging her breasts, she looked at me. There was no void behind those big, sad eyes. What I saw, for the first time, was something so complex, so tragic, that I wanted to walk right over and cover her up with a towel, and apologize, and kiss her hand, and tell her I understood. But I didn't understand, not details, not the stories or history; only the superficial shape that was created by

170

them. My eyes broke our engagement by flitting down below the table again to the light between her legs, flashing on and off like a beacon, and in that moment I realized she didn't want me to embrace her, or apologize, or kiss her hand, or especially to stop looking. She needed my gaze, along with the gazes of hundreds of others. She needed the scandal, the whispers, the surreptitious peeks from men whose wives were preoccupied with tea olives or birdbaths. She wanted to be noticed—in a nutshell that's what it all came down to, the complexity rolled into a concise, verbally expressed human need: Roxy was an orphan.

"Come on," I nudged Mike with my elbow.

We approached the table. Mitch was still sitting beside her on the table, openly staring down her blouse. Boog was leaned against the pole with his hands in his back pockets, half in shade and half out, looking like some recently exhumed, dark-skinned corpse. Reggie sat on the opposite corner of the desk with his back to the others, swinging his leg.

"You about ready?" Reggie said.

"Rox," I said in a cheerful greeting. "And how is Roxy today?"

"Just peachy," she said in her husky, monotone voice.

"Come on," Reggie waved me on. "Tony's liable to be finished."

I saluted her. "So long," I said.

"Bye."

As we were walking back toward the roses I looked over at Reggie. I pushed on his shoulder. "What's with you?"

"Aah?" he said.

"Why you so quiet today; something wrong?"

"Mm?"

"Okay," I said. "Nothing wrong if a guy doesn't want to talk."

"Wha' do you want me to talk about?" Reggie said.

"You mad at Mitch for calling Tony a Dumbo?"

Ballad of the Confessor

Reggie, who had turned his head toward me, turned it back to look straight ahead into the trees that surrounded the nursery. "No," he said.

"You mad at me about something?"

"No."

"You sick?"

Reggie stopped, turned, and put his hand on my shoulder. His small eyes looked out from behind his glasses with a heaviness I'd never seen before. The grin at the corners of his lips seemed a disguise for something.

"Son," he said, "don't take this the wrong way."

"Go on."

"I love you, boy. Don't take this wrong—you hear? The fact is, you'll never know what it's like for us, for me. You might do the work I do, feel the heat the same as me, get as much grief from the boss. But it ain't the same. It just ain't the same. I'm tired, boy. Real tired. I'm tired, and when I look out I see another twenty years of this, if I'm lucky. If I ain't lucky, if my shoulder gives out, or something else breaks down in me, I'm done. Boss'll let me go. Outta work with nothing else I know how to do. I'm tired, I'm just tired. You understand what I'm sayin'? I'm tired is all, and it don't matter. It don't matter if I am tired. It just don't matter."

Reggie took his hand off my shoulder and started walking. His stiff, mechanical walk had always seemed a conspicuous display of brute strength. But I'd been wrong. It was the naked result of moment-to-moment battles with his body and with his faith.

BALLAD OF SYSIPHYS' CHILDREN

There was a pounding on the door. The sound entered my dream, and then became my mother standing outside in the whipping snow, nearly frozen, pounding with her small, frail fists. I called out to her. There was no way to reach her. She kept pounding. The pounding became tapping. The tapping withered and faded into the whistling wind. Then, the pounding returned. I sat up. I heard it again. It was no dream. I got out of bed, pulled on my pants hopping from leg to leg through the bedroom and into the hall.

"Boom—boom—boom."

"Just a minute," I said, reaching back to close the bedroom door. I flipped on the outside light, then looked through the peephole. I saw a figure, small, dark, unfamiliar. I leaned against the door to unlock it, then opened it.

"Rose," I said. There was no need to ask her what she was doing here. She was barefoot. She wore the same shirt she wore yesterday to work. I smelled her booze breath as soon as I opened the door. "Oh, Jesus," I said.

She stood wobbling, stumbling, trying to stay on her feet. The front of her shirt was stained with a big yellow and pink flame-streak.

Ballad of the Confessor

The streak was vomit.

"I. . . I din' mean to bother you," she slurred, her eyes fighting to stay open. "I sorry. . ."

"Rose," I said. When I looked at her I wanted to hit her. I wanted to shove her back and push her down the stairs.

"I sorry," she said again. She made no attempt to leave, or to be asked in.

"When did you start up again?"

"Today. . . No! Ye'erday." She laughed into her hand. "Af'a work, yeah. Yeah, that's right. Af'a work. . ."

"Jesus, Rose."

"Hey," she said with her eyes lit, but then they closed as she appeared to be thinking, or remembering something. "It's okay. Don' worry. Eve'ly thing's all right."

"You working tomorrow?"

"Tomorrow?" She thought about it. Her forehead dimpled. "Yeah," she said.

She was history. The boss wouldn't give her another chance. She'd only been out of rehab for two weeks, and now this. I shook my head. She was utterly hopeless, and it made me mad.

"You need to get some coffee," I said.

"Got any beer?" she chuckled. Her eyes were still closed.

"What time are you supposed to be there?"

"A' work? Mm. . . eight!"

It was nearly two now. There was no way. It was hopeless. "Rose," I said shaking my head looking at her. "Why?"

"Is your wife home?" she said, and her eyes opened suddenly. She moved toward me.

"Come on, Rose," I said, backing away, closing the door so she couldn't get in; her small, rough fingers moved like tentacles along the wood. "Jesus," I said into my arm as the puke smell hit me.

"I gi'. . . gi' you a blow job? You'd like it. Jus' like Mitch. . . an' Boog. . . an' Mike. . . an' Reggie. . .an'. . ."

"Shut up."

"An'. . ."

"I said shut up."

"You."

"*Shhh,*" I told her, then stepped outside closing the door most of the way behind me. "Be quiet."

"Rememba?"

"You're drunk."

I looked behind me through the crack in the door.

"Rememba in the green-*houze,*" she said, and fell against me. I saw it coming and put out my arms. The vomit slick slid against my left hand and forearm. As soon as I pushed her back to where she was, I wiped my arm against the top of her shirt, like a paintbrush on the side of a can.

"You need help," I said, keeping my arms out.

"I like you. I like you mo' than anybody. Youa nice to me."

"Look, Rose," I said.

"You shua you don' got any beer?"

"No, there's no beer."

"Booze?"

"There's nothing. You've had enough. Look at yourself, Rose. Rose. Can I call somebody for you?"

"Call somebody? What fo'?"

"To take you home. You need to get some sleep. Can anybody stay with you? How about Claire; do you know her number?"

Her closed eyes turned belligerent. "Tha' Claire's nothing but a *beetch*. She won' even take me to the movies. I wan'ed to see Tom Hangst. She fucking beetch. Don't better not call *her.*"

"Who then?"

Ballad of the Confessor

"Nobody. Nobody give a damn about *me*." She threw her hand out. It hit the wall hard.

"Christ, Rose," I said. I took her hand and felt it.

"Ow!"

"*Shhhh*. God, Rose, be quiet. I think you fucking broke your hand." I felt it again, behind her second knuckle. There was a break all right.

"*Ow!* That *hurrrrts*." She took her hand away and her stance became defensive. Her head and chest thrust toward me, and her arms flanked her sides. Her eyes remained closed.

"Rose. Rose, can anybody stay with you? I can't. You can't stay here. I'm sorry. I can get you a cab. Rose, maybe the best thing would be to call the police."

"The police!"

"*Shhhh*. Rose, no cabby's going to let you into their cab the way you are. They're closed anyway. Jesus," I said, rubbing my head.

"I can sleep ri' here," she said. She opened her eyes and looked around her. "*Woaaw*. We're up *high*." She took two jerky steps until she came to the wall, then slid down and sat sideways against it. I moved her so she had her back to it. Her hand was already swollen. I thought hard. My thoughts emerged from expedience, then expedience took on a shell of rationalization.

"You stay here, Rose," I said. She was already curling up, oblivious to her hand, or me, or the large moths now congregating around us from the outside light.

I went inside. My wife was standing in the middle of the room. She'd been listening.

"Who's that?" she said bitterly.

"Rose."

"Oh. You mean *that* Rose."

"I'm in no mood. She's drunk. I have to call an ambulance."

"She can't stay here," my wife said with horror.

"She's not staying here. I told you. I'm calling an ambulance."

"Why did she come here?"

"I don't know. She had to go somewhere."

"But why *here*?"

"Don't start."

"What were you doing out there?" She pushed herself toward me in animal aggression as I walked past her.

I began looking for the phone book on the bottom of the rolling cart. I was shaking. She stood over me.

"You were messing around; weren't you?"

"Go to sleep," I said, pretending to ignore her. "Where's the phone book?"

"Weren't you?"

"No."

"Liar."

"Come on. Do you know where it is?"

"I'm going to go right out there and kick her off the porch," she said, and in loud, crushing stomps headed for the door. I leapt up. I ran past her, careful not to touch her, and leaned against the door.

"Don't go out there," I told her. "Leave her alone."

"Why? Afraid she might tell me something?"

"Everything of interest to you, you already know."

"She's a slut. I don't want her on my porch."

"She'll be gone in ten minutes if you'll let me call an ambulance. Why don't you go to bed."

"What's that smell?"

"She threw up."

"Is that what's on your arm? You've got *her* puke on your arm?"

"Look. Why don't you get me the phone?"

"You're a real prick, you know that?"

Ballad of the Confessor

"I'm a prick, I know. Will you just get me the phone?"

"You don't even care, do you?" Her eyes began to well. They welled with self-imposed grief, and with venom. "I hate you."

My heart raced. I felt like I would erupt. "I know you do," I said. "You make it clear every day."

We stood looking at each other. She wiped tears from her eyes, her lip trembling. She approached me, her arm reaching out. I lifted my hands in a defensive posture. She made a gesture of peace with her upturned hand. Then, her hand turned into a fist, and she swung it back. The fist came forward to strike me, but stopped because my hands were ready for it.

"Go to hell," she said through tears.

"I'm there," I answered.

"You, you really are going to hell. Some day. God won't forget. You think you know it all. Well. . ." She left the room. The bedroom door slammed. Long ago, I'd stopped caring that the neighbors heard us. The ugliness of apartment 6B was something I came to accept like some grotesque, incurable disease.

I found the phone book. I sat at the kitchen table, my hands shaking. I marked the spot with my finger. Tears splattered into the deep crease of the phone book. I cried silently so she would not hear me. I closed the book and opened my mouth so I could regulate my breathing, and then stood up wiping my eyes with my palms.

"I'm taking her home," I said as I passed the bedroom door. "That's all I'm doing. You can think what you want."

I opened the front door. Rose was gone. I closed the door behind me and ran down the landing steps. "Rose!" I ran across the grass. "Rose!" I stopped and turned around standing in place. I ran out to the parking lot. I ran between the rows of cars. I ran all the way around our building, looking in the bushes. I ran out to the highway. I looked up, then down it. "Rose!" I came back to the lawn, then went down the embankment that dropped into the dry creek. Lying among strewn heaps of trash, an old refrigerator, a rusted set of mattress springs and a small boat motor, was Rose. Thoughts went through my mind that I would not tell anyone as I slid down the embankment. They were fleeting, but I had them, I can't deny it. Rose had no family. She'd been disowned gradually over the years as her addictions became embarrassments, then dark boils upon the pretty family quilt. She had no real friends. She had collaborators in addiction, but these were not friends in even the most generous sense. She contributed little at work. The boss was kind to have kept her on for so long. She was unreliable, combative, and a mess to look at. She'd spent months in the county jail for repeated drunk driving offenses, had been in and out of rehab several times, and showed no signs of ever coming clean. She was, in short, a nuisance. I looked down on her body. She looked dead already. I asked myself what was the point? Most of those who pity the hopeless deformities of humanity have never had to deal with a Rose. The concept of empathy and compassion are without experience, they're the product of guilt, and fear, and the expectation of non-involvement. What purpose do the Roses of the world serve? They exist for no one's benefit, including their own. Rose was not yet forty, yet she had ten, maybe fifteen years left in her. They'd be years of increasing misery. Like a parasite, she would suck precious days of life from me, and from those who for a period would succumb to guilt or compassion, until the repetitive episodes wore away that guilt or compassion and turned it into cold anger. I looked at her. She was a drunk, liar, whore, thief. I sat her upright. "Rose," I said. *"Rose."* I shook her by the shoulders. I thought of her daughter. I'd never met her. But I thought of *her*; I looked into the puffy, scaly face of Rose and thought of her sleeping, not knowing that her mother was lying drunk in some creek bed.

Ballad of the Confessor

I took handfuls of leaves and mashed them against her shirt, wiping away the vomit. She remained unconscious. I slung her over my shoulder, and staggered up the embankment. As I carried her across the lawn I looked up to the apartment, and there behind the curtain of the sliding glass door saw a shadow. My fear, which had been replaced by resentment and anger, returned, and I hurried along. The back door of the car was unlocked. I opened it and tossed Rose inside, folding her legs in as though she were inanimate. I put my hands in my pockets and realized I didn't have my keys.

"Oh, God," I said. I looked up to the landing and our door. I focused. I tried to remember where I'd left them. They were on the kitchen table. I accounted for the probability that she had moved them. They could be in the drawer, in the nightstand, on top of the refrigerator, or most likely in her hand. I ran across the lawn, up the steps, and opened the door. "I'm taking her to the hospital," I said without looking as I headed for the table. She was standing against the sliding door, staring out the window. The keys were on the table. She made no motion to confront me, and said nothing. "I don't know when I'll be back," I said as I picked up the keys. "Hopefully not long." As I left I felt tremendous relief for having found the keys quickly, and for her non-aggression. But I knew the ease of that moment was not without cause, and that cause was disemboweled love.

THE UNLEASHED
FIREBALLS OF MEN

I was over at Lonnie's helping him put up some drywall. He lives in town not far from Carl's bookshop. He got his house cheap, and some day when all the other places around him are redone, he'll make a fortune on it. There are three stories to the house. It's huge. They don't use the top floor at all. It's just storage now. There's no air conditioning, but Lonnie says it's not bad. He says they have a system where they open all the windows at night to let the cool air in, then in the morning they close everything up to keep the hot day air out. By late in the day it starts to steam up, but it works pretty good he says. He says the worst thing right now are the rats. They come out at dusk, along with the chimney swifts and mosquitoes. They use the wires like a network of roads. He says they'll come right in if you don't have good screens, and all your holes plugged up. He says you get used to it, and after a while you don't look at them the way you did before, as rats; they're just like small, dumb people pouring out of the sewers.

The first winter when the rats started moving inside, Emanuella moved out and lived with some friends until Lonnie shot and poisoned them. He knew he couldn't get rid of them entirely, but he plugged up all the holes and at least diverted them into the walls. She moved back in, and when she heard them running along in the ceiling, he told her they were squirrels. They would only occasionally find a rogue rat who didn't understand the arrangement, and insisted on rummaging through the kitchen garbage can. Lonnie had a pellet gun that he used on the rogue rats; only trouble was, Lonnie wasn't the best shot. They had two cats, but the cats seemed indifferent to the rats and treated them like fellow houseguests. Lonnie said there were times he was aiming at a rat, and he moved the barrel of the pellet gun over to one of the cats instead; but he just couldn't pull the trigger on account of all the grief he'd get from Emanuella. That's when he got Butch. Butch is their dog who's a cross between a poodle and something. He's big for a poodle. Lonnie found him when he was out riding one day. He was all beat-up-looking, and so Lonnie pulled him up on his bike and brought him home. The idea was to nurse him back to health and then find him a good home. But the first time one of those rats came trotting around the corner, Butch was on it. He tore the thing up with a ferocity that made you think there was something personal about it. Butch goes crazy with a rat in his mouth. One time he was thrashing one around, and the thing let loose and flew across the room and hit the antique clock on the wall and broke the glass. Emanuella cursed poor Butch and kicked him and told Lonnie to get rid of him. "Either the dog goes or I go," she said. Lonnie, who likes to kid around, told Emanuella she was making it awful hard on him dropping a big decision like that in his lap, when he just finished deciding between pizza or macaroni and cheese for dinner. Emanuella doesn't like to kid around, and Lonnie's wisecracking gets her yapping and stomping around on the hardwood floors, but Lonnie says it makes for good sex afterwards because she's a little kinky when you get right down to it. He'll force her across the couch when she's still mad and yapping like a little Chihuahua. She'll yelp and howl in her Southern-Portuguese mix, making up all sorts of cuss words Lonnie never heard before; and she doesn't even mind that Butch likes to sit there beside them and watch. Emanuella likes to sunbathe topless in their little courtyard out back. All the people in the houses around the courtyard can see her plain as day. She says Americans are too prudish, that in Portugal all the women sunbathe topless, and some go nude. Lonnie says that's a crock, because when he was over there ten years ago backpacking looking for a wife, he only saw a few topless girls on the beaches, and when he met Emanuella they went to the beach and she always wore a top. She likes the scandal, and that's what burns Lonnie up. She's always yapping about how she'll leave him for Portugal some day, that she's bored in America, that Portugal is so much better. On and on like that. That's why they had Margaret. Lonnie figured if they had a kid she'd have to stick around, and even though he can't take it when she prances around topless and bitches about everything under the sun, he still loves her he says and wouldn't know what to do without her. So he started not using a rubber when they'd have sex, and before you know it along comes Margaret. Emanuella's got high society taste for the housewife of a plastics factory worker. She spends most of her day taking Margaret out window-shopping. Dinner conversation revolves around new drapes and antique chairs; only a little time is spent on Lonnie's crummy day at the factory, and usually Emanuella doesn't hear any of it because she's too busy cutting her snow pea pods into pieces so there's only one pea per bite. But for now Lonnie doesn't mind because he gets to come home and have dinner beside a really primo set of knockers that are usually poking through the gaudy material of Emanuella's skin-tight blouses, and a tight, round little apple ass like you've never seen; then after the baby's down for the evening he'll get her sucked into an argument and start the rough play stuff, and before you know it Butch is sitting there on the fake Persian rug gnawing on Lonnie's boot watching them go at it like two released convicts.

I don't mind doing drywall on somebody else's house; I don't have to be so careful and get uptight if we screw things up. Lonnie said he'd have all the plaster down, but he didn't. You can never trust Lonnie on something like that. He was probably watching *The Honeymooner's* marathon last night instead of tearing down plaster. I don't even mind the demolition part of it. It's shoveling the shit into plastic bags that I hate. All that dust. Of course, Lonnie didn't remember to get masks. I figure four hours of plaster demolition without a mask takes about six months off your lungs. We took a break after hauling the bags of plaster outside so the dust could settle. Emanuella never offers to make lunch when I come over. She's too busy lying in the courtyard, pounding a wedge in the domestic bliss of all the married people in the neighborhood.

"You want to take a peek?" Lonnie smiled at me before we left for lunch. He was standing with his hands on his hips by the window, his hair not combed from this morning, plaster dust weighing it down like snow on leaves.

"What do you mean, do I want to take a peek?" I said. "You mean at Emanuella?"

"You're my best friend. I don't mind if you look."

"Lonnie," I said.

"Come on," he motioned me over by the window.

"You're a fucking pervert."

"Hey," he said. "You'd look if she wasn't my wife."

"Well."

"Well, then come on. I'm giving you the opportunity."

"But it's your *wife*."

"Come on."

184

"What for?"

"Why you being so shy about it?"

"Hell, all right."

I inched my head out the window, so she wouldn't notice me. Emanuella sat in a plastic reclining chair, her hands with their long fingers and chewed nails hanging limp over the armrests, her two long legs brown and smooth and glossy from all the oil she sprayed on them, not crossed, one leg pushed slightly over the other in a sort of languid demureness. Her chest was thrust out like she had words on it she wanted everyone to read. She didn't have words, just the best barbecued breasts in town.

"Hmm," I said.

"Look at her nipples," Lonnie said. "Man, they're pink in the winter. Look at them now. They look like Hershey's Kisses."

"Yeah, they sort of do."

"Pretty nice, aren't they?"

"Sure as shit are."

"Firm too. Man, you wouldn't believe."

"You ready to go?"

"Yeah," Lonnie said tapping his pants pockets in back checking for his wallet. He stuck his head out the window. "Honey? We're leaving. You want us to bring you back anything?" I leaned toward the window, then eased my nose over just enough so I could peek down for a final look. Emanuella had her head tilted up, looking at us from behind a pair of big cheap sunglasses.

"New," she said to Lonnie. She opened and closed her hand in a polite salutation to me.

"How you doing, Emanuella?"

"You don't want us to bring you back a salad or something?"

"Uhh. . ." she thought about it. She winced suddenly, and scratched the side of her left boob; it jostled like a taut water balloon.

185

Ballad of the Confessor

She was just putting on a show. I knew it. Lonnie knew it. They knew I knew it. The fucking perverts. "New," she called up. "I don' thing sew. What time you come back?"

"We'll only be gone an hour. We got a lot to do yet."

"I thing I'll make sawnwich here."

"Okay," Lonnie said. "See you, sweetie."

"See you," I called down, but she ignored me. Butch looked up at us panting. He had a piece of a two-by-four at his feet with chew marks all over it.

We left the house. "Where you want to eat?" Lonnie asked me. The sun cut down from the big droopy fronds of the Palmetto trees, casting prison stripe light on him.

"I don't care," I said. "You buying?"

"Me?"

"Instead of paying me."

"Hell, I just let you look at my wife's naked tits; ain't that worth a day's work?"

"Oh, I see."

"All right, I'll buy. Nothing fancy though."

"A hamburger too steep for you?"

"Depends what kind."

"Just a hamburger."

"You know some place around here?"

"There's a place, Jacque's Café. They're pretty good."

"Okay. But you gotta buy your own beer."

"They don't have beer. It's just a café."

"I'll buy you a Coke. You gotta get your own pie."

"Jesus Christ," I said.

When we got to the café I opened the door and let Lonnie go in first, and then as we were walking toward the counter I made a quick scan of the place looking for the girl, hiding behind Lonnie's sweaty

T-shirt. We sat down. There was a girl making coffee who looked our way.

"Be with you in a second, guys," she said, then banged the filter holder against the trashcan.

We took some menus, which were dirty with dried, wiped food. The counter was dirty too; it hadn't been wiped from the previous customers. Lonnie gave me his look; it's the look he gives me when something's not up to his high society standards. The girl moseyed our way. She lifted her small pad up to her chest and began writing. There was a smear of coffee grounds on her knuckles. "So, you guys know what you want?"

"What's your soup of the day?" Lonnie asked her.

"Chicken noodle."

"How is it?"

"It's okay," she said. "It's not my favorite."

"You mean chicken noodle, or the chicken noodle here?"

"The chicken noodle compared to the other soups. We have a really good cheese broccoli."

"Can I have some of that?"

"Sorry, but we only have chicken noodle today."

"How are your hamburgers?"

"Pretty good," she said.

Lonnie folded up his menu. "I'll just have a hamburger then. Lettuce, tomato, mayonnaise, ketchup—no onions."

"That all?"

"How about some fries."

"Sure. Want something to drink?"

"I'll take a Coke. Put this on one check," he said, arching back stretching like a cat in a weird attempt to impress her. "Okay, slick, get whatever you want. It's my treat."

"I'll have a hamburger too," I said. "Everything on it. No fries for me. Howard Hughes here is on a budget. And a Coke with no ice."

"That all?"

"What are you talking about?" Lonnie said with a phony hurt voice. "I told you, I'm buying. You get whatever you want, pilgrim. I thought you said you were hungry."

"That's all," I said.

"Give the man some fries," Lonnie said. "He's a little shy."

"I don't want fries," I said.

"Give him the fries, really."

"You want fries?" the waitress said. You could tell she was hardly impressed with either of us.

"Okay, if he says so."

"Right," she said, and her little hand smeared with coffee grounds moved over the pad. "You guys want your Cokes now?"

"That'd be sweet of you," Lonnie said with a goofy grin.

"You're five minutes away from your wife, and here you are chatting up the waitress," I said to him after she was gone.

"The trouble with you is, you just don't know how to be a friendly guy," Lonnie said.

The girl from the other day came out between the swinging double doors, adjusting the knot of her apron at the back of her neck. She walked out among the tables and began clearing them, pulling an old cart behind her. The cart had a stuck wheel that made a horrible screech. Lonnie looked over his shoulder toward the noise, then turned back around.

"Place is chock full of bathing beauties," he said sarcastically.

"Yeah," I said without really hearing him. I watched her in the mirror behind the counter. She seemed to move with a sluggishness that wasn't there before. Still, her eyes were bright and her hair, though it was all a mess, was pretty the way it divided around her shoulder when she bent to pick up a stack of dishes.

"You know what?" Lonnie said. He paused, his eyes lurking in the mirror. "I think Emanuella's pregnant again."

"Really?"

"She's not sure, but she missed her period and she's been getting sick in the mornings. That's a pretty good sign."

"You happy about it?"

"Sure I'm happy about it. Maybe this time it will be a boy."

"Is she happy about it?"

"Yeah, she is. She loves children. If it were up to her we'd have ten kids."

"When's it due?"

"Who knows? We don't even know she's pregnant for sure. She's settling down. She doesn't talk about moving back to Portugal as much. I think she knows I treat her good." The waitress brought us our Cokes. I took the tip of the straw wrapper and balled it up with the tips of my fingers. I kept rolling it around and around. "You know, she wouldn't be so bad if she'd smile a little," Lonnie said, following our waitress with his always-searching, rover's eyes.

"Maybe she's having a bad day," I said. "Isn't she allowed to have a bad day?"

"Sure. But when you're a waitress you better pretend like it ain't."

My girl, who I'd been carefully following in the mirror, began pushing the cart now full of dirty dishes toward the far end of the counter. The wheel skidded in agony.

"That girl's going to lose those dishes," I said. I got up and hurried over. I arrived just as the tall stack of plates began wobbling. "Let me help you," I said. I steadied the plates, then took half of them in my hands and put them on the lower shelf of the cart. The girl, whose hair had been sloshing like car wash rags in her face, brushed it back and looked up at me.

189

Ballad of the Confessor

"Hey," she said, smiling. "How are you doing?"

"Pretty good," I said. She looked more like I remembered. "Looks like you need a new wheel."

"That cart's been that way since I've been here," she said, taking the hair on the left side of her face and curling it behind her ear. Her fingers lingered around the lobe, then moved down her neck to her collarbone where she rubbed it unconsciously.

"How's it been going?" I asked her. I felt like I was standing in somebody else's body.

"Not bad."

"Yeah?"

"Yeah; how about with you?"

"Pretty good. I went to the beach a couple Sundays ago. I went fishing over on Sullivan's Island. You been going?"

"Not in the past two weeks."

"Been busy, eh?"

"I guess so," she shrugged. She looked as though she wanted to let something out, but she couldn't.

"Where do you go?"

"You mean what beach?" She hesitated, then tilted her head up. Suddenly, she seemed to be in deep thought. "Oh, I go to different ones. I don't like crowds."

"Me neither. I fish mostly. You do any fishing?"

"I go with my dad sometimes."

"You ever go to Sullivan's Island?"

"I go there all the time," she said. "Is that where you go?"

"Pretty much. There's a good spot near Fort Moultrie."

"Does your wife go with you?"

"My wife?"

"You're married, aren't you?"

"Yeah," I said. "But my wife doesn't like to fish." I dropped my head and kicked at the floor. "I don't know. . ."

"What is it?"

"I don't know. It's just that—" I looked up at her. "Things aren't going so good," I said.

"Why not?" Her voice changed. It took on a low huskiness.

"She basically hates me. She thinks I'm an asshole. She's ashamed of me."

"Why would she be ashamed of you?"

I pinched my grubby T-shirt. "This is as good as I get," I told her. "There's nothing more."

"I'd never be ashamed of you," she said. When she spoke those words it was as if the whole room changed from black and white to color. My perceptions of her, and of myself, exploded. It changed what I allowed myself to think and say to her.

"Listen," I began, but then hesitated. "Aw, I know you're busy. I'm sorry."

"No," she said, and then she touched my arm. "What is it?"

"Well, I'll be fishing in my usual spot next Sunday. If you're not doing anything. . ."

"What time?"

"I usually get there about nine."

"I'm not sure," she said. Her eyes moved back and forth between mine, searching for sincerity. Her hand closed tighter, as though she were fighting a pain that was passing through her. "I'll try to make it. I want to," she said, and then let go of my arm.

"Okay," I said, drifting away from her. "See you later."

"Bye," she said. The howling of the wheel tore through the place like a jackhammer.

"What's with you?" Lonnie said as I returned to my swivel seat.

"What do you mean?"

"You and the girl?"

Ballad of the Confessor

"I was just helping her, then we got to talking." Our hamburgers came. I picked mine up and took a bite. I knew he was still looking at me, waiting for a better answer. "I'm just being a friendly guy," I said.

She came out from the kitchen twice before we finished eating, once to look for a rag. She found one, then stood before us moving it from hand to hand like it was a Slinky. "What's your name?" she said.

"Lorne."

"Lorne? That's different."

I was chewing. I took a sip of my Coke through the straw, then trying to be all casual and cool in front of Lonnie said, "Yeah, well you don't get to choose your own name, do you?"

"I'm Emily. I thought you should know that." She turned and walked back through the swivel doors into the kitchen. Before she went through the doors she looked back and waved.

Lonnie looked at me straight-faced.

"What?" I said.

He was giving me the straight-faced tease.

"You ready?" I got up from my seat.

He sat without moving, smirking.

"Come on, big spender. Yeah, and you better keep your mouth shut too."

On our walk back Lonnie talked about the factory and everything that was going on there, but I wasn't listening. I was thinking of Emily. Lonnie won't ever know it, but that walk was a cyclone of emotions for me. I had only felt that way once before. It was the day I got my cast removed from my arm when I was twelve years old.

THE SHATTERING

Antoinette started the other day because Jim quit. I heard Jim got an engineering job in Columbia. Antoinette is Russian. Her Russian name isn't Antoinette. She won't tell anybody what it is. She changed it when she came to America. She's tiny. She doesn't do any lifting, and very little labor in general. She was hired for her cheap intellect, like Jim. There's talk that the boss thinks she's even smarter than Jim, which would make her smarter than me; but I can tell you, she's not going to be around too long, so she doesn't really count.

The boss hired her to redesign the nursery. He explained how he wanted everything in a logical place. Things had to be logical in relation to being unloaded from the trucks, in relation to their ease of moving, in relation to their preference for sun or shade, in relation to visibility for customers, and in relation to other complimentary items. She spends most of the time in trailer A where the boss' office is. I heard she has some fancy software package to help with the redesign. Reggie says she doesn't know beans about plants, but that the boss doesn't care about that. He figures you don't have to know plants to redesign a nursery. Hell, you might as well be redesigning a putt-putt golf course. When you're making up the chart you don't

193

Ballad of the Confessor

call things by name anyway; you call them A or B, or X or Y, or 1 or 2. In fact, it just confuses matters to call them azaleas, or tea olives, or red-hot pokers, or God forbid Primula denticulata. You use things called parameters, and it's the parameters that really count. A or B or Primula denticulata—it just doesn't matter. Just make sure you got your parameters and you know what they are. That's what Reggie says the boss says. Sometimes she's not in the trailer. She sits on the bench nearest the shitters and draws rows of little boxes on the master plan. Everybody is curious how the master plan is going to affect them. We all stop and look over her shoulder and ask her all kinds of questions. She's very polite, and always takes the time to give us answers. Eddie is over there the most. He likes any kind of drawing. You'll see him drawing in the dirt with a stick when he's sitting out under the big tree waiting for his ride. He likes her accent, the way we all do, but mostly it's because he's fascinated by the master plan.

Yesterday I sat down with her on the bench. I asked her if it would be all right if I ate my lunch with her.

"Oh, shore," she said, "there's plenty ov room."

She had the big sheet of paper on a board. The drawing looked like an aerial view of a city with wavy lines, green blobs that were trees, outlines for the buildings, a blue blob that was the pond; but most of the plan was a grid of squares, each square filled with different letters or numbers. She had that constipated look of someone in the middle of taking an exam.

"You ever do this before?" I asked her.

"Never," she smiled. When she smiled her cheeks balled up like little biceps.

"Where are we?"

She put her finger on the spot, a small rectangle beside two small squares. I put my hand to my chin and tapped my mouth with my finger.

"How's everything going to get into all those squares?" I asked her.

"I guess sambady will have to move them," she said.

I gave a sigh and sat back. I opened up my paper bag and pulled everything out and set them on the flat arm of the bench, then folded up the paper sack neatly and tucked it underneath my leg. I asked her where she was from. She told me some name I'd never heard of and knew I'd never remember. "It's a bleak oondustrial city near Moscow," she said. When she said *near* she meant the way Charleston is *near* Washington D.C.

"Why'd you come over here?" I asked her.

She looked at me with a startled, but amused reaction. "We arrived before the wall came down," she said. "We fled the country."

"You fled? You mean you were dissidents?"

"Exactly. We were dissidents."

"So, you and the KGB were buddies."

"Boosum buddies," she said. "You can't imagine how boosum we were."

For the next, I listened as she told me her story. She was young when she met her husband. He was a man bigger than life, she thought. Big physically, with a big ego and charisma to match. He drew her in with his passionate words against communism and the party. He was an engineer, but became bored with it and went to school for physics. He taught for a while, and then he thought it would be a good idea to learn how to drive, so he became a taxi driver. After that he made unheard of money facilitating the movement of illegal machinery up north. She was so in love, she said, that he was all she thought of day and night.

They got married. Her husband had begun to join in demonstrations against the government. His goal was to make noise directed at the outside world, in hopes of being let out of the country. She began to help him. The Afghan War made tensions between the Soviet and American governments worse. They moved to Riga on the Baltic Sea for a better chance of escaping. Riga is such a beautiful city, she said. There was no such thing as a vacant apartment in those days. To move, you had to arrange a switch. Nobody wanted to move to their city, but luckily someone had to move there to look after a relative. The apartment in Riga was small, with more people in it. But it didn't matter. They were in *Riga*. The press knew about them, the *Western* press. The KGB couldn't just arrest everybody they wanted, because it would make the Western papers. They had to remove dissidents discretely. Half the time they sent you out of the country, and half the time you were sent to Siberia. "It was a gamble," Antoinette said, "and we lost." Her husband, Dimitri, was sent to Siberia.

"There was a trial, of course. We had no money for lawyers, and besides, you could not find a lawyer who would stand up to the government anyway. So I became his lawyer. That's right. Me. They could not stop me—the law permitted it. I read all I could, but it was hopeless. The day of the trial we had two busloads of witnesses, but then they told us we could not use them. I said, what do you mean we can't use them? And they said, you can't use them. So I see what is happening. It is obvious it is all a big charade. So I ask to see Dimitri, and then I tell him what is happening, that he is going to Siberia no matter what, it is certain. I tell him I want to protest, to walk out, to not participate in the charade they are orchestrating. Dimitri, sadly, agreed with me. So, that is what we did. We walked out. As soon as the trial started and the judges brought everyone to order, I made the statement of protest, and we all walked out. Dimitri was sent to prison.

"He was there for three years. During that time, I increased my activism. I attended political rallies, and any other kind of internationally covered event. The KGB followed me wherever I went. In springtime they followed me for several weeks straight, taking photographs of all my outfits. They'd pass by holding their small box camera, supposedly in disguise, and then without raising it up or without them looking at me, they'd snap the picture. It was so obvious. I mean, come on. You can see the lens reflecting light and you can hear the *click* that the camera makes; who do they think they're fooling? Such clowns, the KGB. I would go see him. I took the train—such a long ride through the bleak Siberian countryside. When I would see him we would be like animals after not being together for so long. We would maul each other like dogs; I didn't care who saw or heard. Dimitri was often agitated, and angry that I was not doing enough to get his release. I told him, 'Dimitri, I am doing everything I can, but it's not easy opposing the government.' His mind turned against him, not all the time, but sometimes. He wondered if I really wanted him to stay in prison; and of course he suspected I had a lover.

"The KGB, they were both buffoons and serious killers. They thought they were just doing their job. None of them really believed the propaganda of communism; it was a matter of survival, like it was for everybody else. They took me on several occasions and scared me with threats. They were on every bus, train, plane, and behind every building. The only way I could face them was to pretend to both them and myself that they didn't scare me. I lashed out at them, or laughed at their ridiculous surveillance techniques. I was not alone. I had a friend whose brother was also in prison. We became like sisters. Without each other, I think we would have perished.

"One night I was supposed to meet someone. The place was far away from the city at a train stop. Train stops in Russia are not like

Ballad of the Confessor

they are here; this was nothing—a broken down shack in the middle of the wilderness. I take a taxi to the spot and wait for the man. I believe he has news from Dimitri, and may aid in our release from the country. But it was all a hoax, a setup. There was no man, no meeting. Another KGB game. So here I am in the wilderness—it's winter—and it's dark now, and I have no way of getting home. These young men came up to me. They had been standing off to the side like vultures for hours. What could I do? You don't understand. They wanted to rape me. It was clear. Perhaps they even wanted to kill me afterward. I tried to think of a way out. They began teasing me; there was real hunger in their eyes. I told myself that the only way out was to find the one person, the one weak link, who I could gain sympathy from. So, I made eye contact with this man. The one who would save my life. I stood closer to him, and flirted in a way. He became protective, as I had hoped. Eventually, he led me away to his farm. He turned out to be a good man, with a wife and daughter. They treated me with kindness and let me stay over night. In the morning he drove me back to the city. But he just as easily could have raped, and then killed me.

"They finally let Dimitri out of prison. It was so unbelievable! Oh, my! On a flight back to Riga, months before, the KGB man all but admitted we had beaten them. He says, 'You think you have won. If you want the truth, I wish we had never gotten involved with you. We should have let you go two years ago. But. . .' And then this man, he says the most awful thing. He looks at me and smiles. 'You won't be together. You may have beaten us. You'll get out of the country. You'll go to America. But you won't be together.' I think, *What do you mean we won't be together?* I'm looking at this big stupid KGB man who thinks he knows something and I laugh at him. I am this young woman, so in love. So in love, I can't tell you how much. And here is this man telling *me* I won't be with my husband in

America? I thought he was crazy. But you know what? That was the only thing the KGB ever told me that turned out to be true."

"You said your husband was tortured," I said. "What did they do to him?"

"Well, first of all it's Siberia. The cold alone, that is torture. He would write me letters and tell me about the cold, how in winter he sometimes thought he would freeze to death and they would find him in the morning frozen solid. My husband, he is no pacifist. He makes trouble for himself. Whenever he would get into trouble, they would put him in a small room all by himself for two weeks. Two, sometimes three. Whatever they decided. They're the bosses. Feeding him very little during this time. They could beat him whenever they wanted. I went to see him many times. It is amazing how much information you can get from people. I became an expert at getting bits of information out of people on trains—people I didn't even know. I would just start talking. And then they would talk too. It's boring on those long train rides. Before you know it, they're saying things about people I know. My husband was even better. He got even the prison guards to give him information. Even they liked him.

"When he got out we were given three days to get out of the country. We didn't waste time. We went first to Israel, then came here. The people who helped us get out, they took us around like we were on tour. Like celebrities. We would go to these dinners and give speeches. We met very important people. Millionaires, even billionaires. We went to this one reception at this billionaire's penthouse. It was so boring. When we are ready to leave the billionaire who is just in town for a few hours said we should ride together to the airport. So he gets the limousine with us and you know what? He made us pay half! Ha! Here is this billionaire with all this money and he says he never carries money and that we should split the cost. My husband hated that. His English was not so good after spending three years in prison, and he was still in the beginning stages of psychological recovery. He had so much to adjust to. His new life out of prison. A new country. A wife that was now independent. He is a proud man, a macho type of man. He didn't like my independence at all. He wanted me the way I was before he went to prison, but of course I wasn't the same person I was before he went to prison. What could I do?

"He went to university to become a lawyer, and I worked. We had our son. Even then the marriage was failing." Antoinette paused a moment to reflect. "I think it was because before there was this enemy, communism, the KGB, the games we played, and there was a purpose. When we finally got out, we had won. But now there was no enemy anymore, no great goal that we were striving for. There was only us, and we, or at least I, had changed.

"We drifted farther and farther apart and then, believe it or not, he was the one who left me. Yes. It's true. He said he didn't want me anymore because I was too independent for him. He felt very threatened. He is the most macho man and he doesn't like anyone, especially his wife, competing with him. Now, five years later, we are still not divorced. You know why?" Antoinette smiled broadly and shook her head. "Games, games, games. All the silly games. I loved to play them too. But now I don't play them. I'm through with games. He still wants to play, but me, I want no more games in my life. I've had enough."

I walked around for the next ten minutes under the blasting sun, my head clouded, my eyes burning looking into the shady parts of the nursery beneath the trees. Everything seemed washed out. I kicked a rock as I went shuffling in zigzags, thinking about the wild story Antoinette told me. I felt small. My problems seemed small, my world seemed small. It made me mad that I was so small. I looked out through the fence to the highway, across it to the Kwik Mart where Reggie gets his pop and potato chips and candy bars. All the new development going on around us swirled in my head like some stirred up mug of poison. What was I doing here? I held my head and slid down the trunk of a tree—it was so hot. I'm not living a life, I thought to myself; I'm using it up. That's what I'm doing. Why couldn't I be Antoinette's macho husband who fought against communism when it was still dangerous to do it, then be sent to Siberia for three years where my tiny but lion-hearted wife wrote letters to Western newspapers and was followed every day by the KGB taking pictures of her spring outfits so they could recognize her wherever she went, and traveled thousands of miles by train to come see me for conjugal visits where I'd rip off her pants in the cold, filthy cell of my existence the moment she arrived—and pummel her against the gritty face of the three-hundred year old, profanity-splattered wall so she gasped and moaned, filling the halls of the prison with the sound of female pleasure and release and song, the rest of the prisoners banging on the bars of their cells with metal cups, clapping, cheering, pushing their sunken, scabby faces between the bars closer to the dream that was happening only inches away.

I felt ashamed and wanted to hide from Antoinette. I knew I was nothing compared to her. I dug at the ground with a flat, wafer-sized rock. She was like the arrival of Tony. Tony, who broke through the stone confines of strength set by Lyle. Lyle, who had shattered my perceptions of strength, when he could be motivated to work, set by Reggie. Reggie, who showed me that first day unloading the big semi full of plant material from California, what real physical labor was. There had been perception, then the shattering of it. A new perception, and the shattering of it. With each shattering, my own limitations were illuminated more clearly. There was nowhere to hide against such stark nakedness. I knew where I fell in comparison. It sucked out my courage. It drained me of enthusiasm. It seemed the

Ballad of the Confessor

world was at an end, but I knew it wasn't, and because it wasn't I'd have to face each day those who soared, while I hobbled along like some hapless imbecile. How does the sleek, new world-appetite of youth disintegrate into the piecemeal pseudo-existence of the rest of your life? I rubbed my eyebrows, then my whole face. I got up. I slapped the fronts of my jeans and watched them puff with peat moss dust. The only way I could move away from the tree was to tell myself that Antoinette had her experiences, Tony had his Hercules strength, but I had something else, something neither of them had, something even Reggie could not quite comprehend or ever acquire: I have the torment of unrealized, inextinguishable hope. I am the anonymous wind howling through canyons.

THE SECOND MAN

I stood with my eyes closed against the boss' trailer, around the corner so nobody could see me. Everybody knew where I was, but I didn't want them to see me. My eyes twitched rapid-fire. I kept thinking I could go back and undo it all, but I couldn't, and I got sucked into the sidetrack thought of why I couldn't. Reggie opened the door and looked around the corner at me.

"Boss wants to see you now," he said, then his head disappeared.

I stepped from behind the trailer. Everybody was hovered around, pretending not to be watching, when that's exactly what they were doing. I walked in and shut the door behind me. It was nice and cool in the air-conditioned office. Antoinette had been working in the office, but the boss asked her to leave ten minutes earlier. She was sitting on the bench near the shitters pretending to be working on the master plan, when I knew she was watching just like everybody else. This was something you couldn't help watching, even if you weren't the nosy type by nature.

The boss sat behind his desk cluttered with wrenches, papers, and dirt. Antoinette kept the desk clean; it didn't take the boss but ten minutes to dirty it back up. The customer who had the complaint against me sat in the ripped up naugahyde chair, the cushiest chair by far in the office, to the boss' right. Reggie sat to her right, just inside the door, facing them. There was an empty chair for me beside Reggie.

"Have a seat, Lorne," the boss said as I came in. The usual flatness of someone who's always preoccupied with ten different thoughts at once was gone from his long, gray-copper face. He appeared to be focused solely on this meeting; his long forearms were in his lap, instead of on the table the way he usually had them. "Lorne," he said, "I've talked with Mrs. Baker. She told me what happened. She says you said some bad things to her. Is that true?"

"I said some things I probably shouldn't have said," I said.

"Haww," quipped Mrs. Baker like a bird, and looked out the small, smeared-dirt window.

"She said you called her some names." The boss hesitated. Seriousness was plastered all over his face. "I won't repeat what they were. Did you call her those names?"

"Yes sir," I said. "I think so. I mean, if we're talking about the same names."

"I see."

"He's been working enough for two men," Reggie said plainly to the boss, then his small eyes moved to Mrs. Baker. "It don't excuse him, but he's been overworked, the boy has."

The boss listened to Reggie carefully. Everything about the boss was calculated and grave, and I knew I was in serious trouble. "Lorne," the boss turned again to me. "We'll discuss your situation here at the nursery in a minute. But right now I'd like you to apologize to Mrs. Baker. I've explained to her that we value our customers here at the nursery. I told her how you're one of the best workers we have. I don't know what got into you, but whatever it is we don't stand for that kind of behavior—not even once. Lorne," he said, and showed me the way to Mrs. Baker with his big leathery hand.

I was trembling. I wanted to be anywhere but there. I looked at Mrs. Baker. I wanted to poke her eyes out. I felt sorry for her. I thought what it would feel like to take a two-by-four to her legs. "Mrs. Baker," I said, "I really didn't mean it, what I said. I've been having a bad time of it lately. I don't know, I think it all hit me at once, and I took it out on you. I'm sorry. There's no excuse, I know. It's hot working out here all day. Real hot. I know that doesn't excuse me. Well, I don't know what else to say. I hope you won't hold it against the boss here, or the nursery. This is the finest place to work in all of Charleston, and the best nursery too. I hope you'll find it in your heart to forgive me."

Mrs. Baker didn't say a thing. She'd been boring a hole into my forehead with her gray, gorilla eyes, but now looked out the window again with a nervous sigh; her foot tap-tap-tapped against the leg of the metal desk. I think she wanted out of there as much as me.

"Reggie, will you walk Mrs. Baker to her car?" the boss said. Reggie stood up with mechanical slowness and opened the door for Mrs. Baker. I heard her sandals slap against the metal steps.

The boss sat back in his folding chair with his hands behind his head. He looked at me with heavy eyes. After some time I figured he wanted me to say something.

"I'm really sorry," I said with a shrug.

"She said you called her a pinhead in a girdle."

"Maybe," I said vaguely, looking up. "I can't remember exactly what I said."

"She said you called her a tapeworm with a marble for a brain."

"Well. . ."

"She said you said you were going to hack off her toes with a mattocks if she didn't high tail it on outta here."

"I know," I said dropping my head. "I know."

Ballad of the Confessor

"What the hell happened?" the boss said, and his big hands came down in two separate thuds on the desk.

"I don't know."

"Reggie said, in your defense, that Mrs. Baker said something about Tony. Is that true?"

"Yeah, she did," I told him.

"Would you mind telling me what she could possibly have said to make you say those horrible things?"

"She called him an idiot."

"An idiot."

"That's right."

"What did Tony do to prompt her to call him an idiot?"

"Nothing."

"Reggie said Tony was loading roses onto her cart, when he let go of one and it landed on her foot."

"He gets nervous around her type."

"So she called him an idiot? I talked to Tony. He didn't say anything about it. How come if it's okay with Tony, it's not okay with *you*?"

"Come on, boss," I said. "Don't make me spell it out for you."

"I don't want to let you go, Lorne. But I may have to." He lifted his hands and came forward in the chair and set his big forearms on the desk. "I'm giving you every chance possible to save your job," he said.

"I know. I'm sorry I said what I said. But you weren't there. You didn't see the look she had for Tony. Even if she hadn't said anything, she deserved it for that look."

He studied me. I felt my face hot with blood. I felt like a damn fool. "Okay, Lorne," he said standing up. His mind was shifting into high gear again. "You're off tomorrow, right? Come in Monday morning and I'll let you know what I decide. Anything else you want to say?"

"No."

"Tell Antoinette she can come back in. You and Reggie get those yews moved before the truck comes in." He looked at his old Timex watch. "Should be here by two." I stood up, glad to be needed again. "Have a good weekend, Lorne. Think things over. Give me a call at home if you want."

I left the office and when the bright broiling sun hit me I felt sick. I walked past Roxy's desk where Mitch and his gang were hanging out. They all stopped their talking and watched me pass—not a wise-crack from any of them. I passed the twin shitters; the smell made me want to puke. Antoinette looked up as I approached her. Where everyone else looked at me with pitiful, gloomy expressions, she had her cheeks balled up in the little muscles, like she was deciding whether to bust out laughing or congratulate me.

"Well?" she said. "How did it go?"

"About how you could expect it to go."

"Did you get the shit-can?"

"I won't know until Monday."

"Tell me about it," she said.

I sat down next to her, feeling weary and hot. "Got it all figured out?" I asked her, nodding toward the big sheet of paper.

"This? Oh! It's nothing. . . Tell me, unless you don't want to. Did you really bite the woman?"

"Who told you that?"

"Mitch and Roxy were talking."

"No, I didn't bite her."

"Lorne," she said leaning into me placing a hand on my arm, "why did you do it?"

"It's really strange. It happened so fast. It was just a reaction. I didn't plan on doing it. It just came out."

Ballad of the Confessor

"I understand," she said. "I completely understand."

I got up. When I looked down on her small, big-eyed figure I wanted to ask her why she understood, when I didn't understand it myself. But it was useless. "Boss says you can come in now," I told her. I shuffled away without saying anything else. I heard the sound of the tractor being started across the nursery, muffled by the sound of clicking, spitting sprinklers, and the laboring cough of a truck on the highway. I saw the trees bending in the breeze, and Evelyn's white hair in the shade. She held up her hand and waved. Beneath the swaying whites of the overturned leaves she looked frail and ghostlike. I walked toward her. It seemed like I was heading into a tunnel, with an apparition floating wide-armed in the distance. Her fingertips were dark with soil, her eyes muddied with cataracts. I dragged a new bag of peat moss to her potting bench and opened it for her.

"Anything else I can do?" I asked her.

"No," she said, "but thank you."

"Okay. See you later."

"Don't let it get to you, Lorne."

"The thing is, it only gets simpler the more I think about it," I said. "Isn't that strange?"

"Will you go to Colorado?"

"We'll see."

"Will she go with you?"

"It's hard to say."

"You've been a good worker," she said to me. "We'll all miss you if you don't come back."

"I'll make sure Reggie gets somebody to look after you."

"You're a good man."

"Not really."

"There's more to life than this nursery. There's more than Colorado. There are things you can't imagine. Remember that when you don't feel so good." I leaned over and kissed her. I felt odd for doing it. I'd probably see her Monday morning same as usual.

I passed Tony, who was with Reggie loading up the trailer with mulch. He stopped working. His big mountain of a body expanded and contracted with each breath; sweat blotched his T-shirt and ran in free tracks down his red face. He fidgeted around, moving his big shoulders and shifting his weight from one foot to the other. Reggie clamored over the mulch pile and came up to me.

"Lorne," he said. "Well?"

"Well, I don't know."

"Boss is pretty mad, ain't he."

"Yeah, he's pretty mad all right."

"You tell him what the lady said about the nursery?"

"No."

"Son," Reggie said shaking his head.

"What's the use?"

"What's the use? Don't you want to save yourself? Boss knows how you like it here. He knows how you care about everybody here. She might as well have slapped you in the face. Lorne," Reggie seemed to be begging me.

"It doesn't matter," I said.

"You at least tell him what she said to Tony?"

"Yeah."

"What'd he say?"

"He said it didn't bother Tony, so why should it bother me."

Reggie kept shaking his head, making me feel dumber. "Don't you think he'd look at it different if he knew?"

"You better not say anything," I said.

"I ain't."

"You better not."

Ballad of the Confessor

"I ain't."

"Okay then."

"Maybe you wanna lose your job," Reggie seemed to be thinking out loud. "Maybe that's why."

"It's not that complicated," I said.

"I know. That's why I say maybe you wanna lose your job."

"I'd rather nobody knew, that's all."

He put his big hand on my shoulder. "You come to my church some day?"

"Maybe I will."

"We can still go fishing."

"We better."

"Come to church this Sunday?"

"I don't know. Let me think about it."

"I'll be there every Sunday. No matter what else happens, I'll be there every Sunday."

"Watch the potato chips," I said putting my hand on his big, hard stomach. "You sure there ain't somebody in there?"

"What're you doing now?"

"Nothing. Boss said we better move the yews before the truck comes in."

"Awhh," Reggie said hitting himself in the head with his fist. "I forgot all about 'em."

"You want me to move them?"

"Naw." He swung around waving his hands. "Tony! Tony—hold up! Stop loading!" He turned back around. "Me and Tony'll dump this load, then meet you at the yews."

"Okay," I said. I started heading back toward the yews. I heard the engine on the tractor whine, then catch and hum. The yews were near the front of the nursery. I cut through the concrete statuary and fountains, my feet heavy wearing those big, blocky boots. I started moving the yews, grasping them by their foliage three in a handful. I wasn't thinking about losing my job anymore. I couldn't think about anything, except the mechanical process of moving the yews, fast, before the truck came in. That's when I saw the second man. Not the one who carries the cross, but the man who talks to himself. He walks north, in the opposite direction as the man who carries the cross, on the same side. The second man wears dark blue slacks and a white shirt. He looks like an altar boy. He talks to himself gesticulating, as if he were making some very important point to someone. But no one is ever with the man. He is always alone. He carries a book in his hand. He'll have the book shoved in his face as he walks, and then it appears he is reading from the book. I watched him. It was then I was crushed, not by the tragedy, but the comedy. I watched him disappear, his hands flapping, his head darting in all the most ridiculous angles.

SACRED SOJURN

When I was down the side of the gully with Rose, I noticed an old bicycle among the trash heaps and knocked-over appliances. Saturday morning I went down and fished out the bike. Everything about it was okay, except for the front wheel which was warped. The tire was flat with a pinkie-sized hole in the tube. I pushed the bike down to K-Mart and bought a new tube. I asked the frizzy-haired lady working in the toy section if I could return the tube if it didn't work out. I explained to her how bad the rim was and that maybe the tire, once the tube was inflated, wouldn't stay on. She was a heavy breathing, wheezing sort of person. I seemed to be bothering her, although there weren't but a few people in the toy section. I pushed the bike to the gas station across the street, fit the new tube in the tire, and blew it up. When the tire was nice and hard I bounced it on the ground. I put the tire back on the bike keeping it upside-down, and cranked the pedal and made the wheel go around fast. The wheel kept hitting the brake. I opened up the brake as far as it would go with a stick, but the wheel still rubbed against it. I poked my head inside the garage and asked the kid there if he had a wrench I could borrow. He said sure and pointed to his toolbox. I found a wrench

212

and removed the brake pads. I tested the wheel again and it didn't hit anything. Now I wouldn't have any front brakes, but that was okay because I wasn't going to be going that fast anyway.

I started riding along the highway. The clouds up in the sky were like a sheet of cracked, white earth, and the dimness gave everything a feel of uncertainty. I stayed over on the cinders and dirt and high grass, away from the speeding traffic. I rode toward the crabbing dock. The parking lot was nearly empty. There were two women standing in the water tossing nets unenthusiastically into the muddy river; maybe they were testing out new nets, or practicing. I put the bike down and walked out onto the dock.

"Hey," I nodded to the only two guys on the dock, who sat toward the Cooper River Bridge smoking sitting with fishing poles between their legs. They sort of nodded at me. "Catching anything?" The one guy ignored me, but the other guy with bloodshot eyes shook his head.

"Not nothin'," he said.

"Least it ain't too hot," I said. I went out to the end of the dock and put my hand on the post that was white as an old bone, all cracked and smeared with dried fish guts and splattered with gull shit. I picked up a hollow crab claw and made it open and close, open and close, open and close, then tossed it onto the water and watched it float and wobble in the small, happy cup-waves, then a gull who'd been circling me went down for it but pulled up before snatching it out of the water because he knew without touching it what it was. I got down on my stomach and looked under the dock for crabs clinging to the posts. I stared into the water. The tide was going slowly out. A turtle poked his head up ten feet out and I thought it was a snake at first. The turtle watched me, then disappeared.

"See you later," I said to the two guys fishing as I stepped around

Ballad of the Confessor

them. They both sort of bobbed their heads. I rode back along the winding dirt and cinder road toward the highway, stopping to look into the marsh water over the small bridges. The sheet of clouds was breaking up, but there was still no sun of any consequence. I was back on the highway riding again. I knew Mike played soccer Saturdays on a field nearby. I found the field, some beat up lumpy patch of too-tall grass with one still-standing goal at one end, and nothing at the other end. They put two balled up piles of shirts at the empty end for a goal. They were all Mexicans. Seven shirted Mexicans on one side, and eight shirtless Mexicans on the other side. Mike was nowhere to be seen. I watched until they took a water break, and then I rode over and asked if Mike played with them. They said he did but he wasn't here today. They asked me if I played and I said I did but I only had these sandals on. They said come back sometime with shoes on and play. There were some pretty young Mexican girls among the sweaty Mexican players. They wore shorts and colorful shirts and they all had the longest darkest hair like horses tails, and the darkest eyes. I stayed a while listening to everybody talk in Spanish. Finally, I got my bike going and made a turn back for the highway, and the one who'd asked me if I played shouted good-bye in English, and waved even while he was guarding somebody and running.

There stood the mighty Cooper River Bridge. Suddenly, for no reason, I thought of my wife sitting back at the apartment alone, or at the beach alone, or shopping alone, and in the cloudy stillness of the late Saturday morning it made me fold in on myself with heartache and sadness and all sorts of promises to myself that I knew I'd never be able to keep. I shifted the bike into low gear. The gears worked fine. My legs went round fast but it was easy pedaling, and the view was spectacular because I was above the wide band of the metal guardrail. I stopped and looked out over the river side toward the crabbing dock and I saw the two dots on it that were the two guys fishing, but couldn't see any other dots in the water and figured the women crabbing must have gone home. The clouds had broken up and were now like castaway icebergs off on their own and the sun had room to shine, then not shine, then shine some more. I walked the bike up farther to the very top. I looked straight down. It was a long way to the river. Every year people jump off the bridge into the river. Some of them live, and some don't. They're all trying to get free.

I leaned my bike against the guardrail and put my forearms on the thin, cutting edge, and looked at the wide crescent-glare stretching from one side of the river to the other. I know my brain is full of memories, but standing there I couldn't think of any. It needs things to jar them loose. I climbed up so I was standing on the guardrail, holding onto the thick support beams with both hands. I heard the sound of honking cars, and people hollering but not stopping. I looked down. The muddy-green of the river moved in slow twinkles. It was too hard looking down, so I looked up to the clouds breaking apart into white icebergs floating on the blue-gray sky with white light pouring down onto the curved pie slice of earth. I saw the two dots on the dock enlarge. They were standing up—they'd seen me. I saw the dots move, but couldn't tell what sort of movements they were, whether they were urging me, or trying to dissuade me, or doing neither and were lost in the chaotic waning of the morning the same as I was. I stuck my fist out toward them. I pumped it hard. My right side tensed with adrenaline. The whole wide river mouth was beautiful, and it hurt to see it all. I felt my own smallness.

When I turned, slowly, shuffling my feet inch-by-inch, there was a crowd of people forming around me. Two men rushed up and took me by my arms. They wouldn't let go. I told them to get their filthy mitts off me, but they wouldn't. They had such sorrowful,

Ballad of the Confessor

determined scowls. I sank my teeth into the shoulder of one tormentor—he howled and let go.

"I'm not going to jump!" I told them for the third time.

The guy who was still holding my right arm freaked out when he saw his friend's bleeding shoulder. He backed off. Some of the people left, while others stood stunned or disappointed. I got my bike and walked it through the mob, then when I was away from them I climbed on and began riding again. People stared at me as they drove by. The guy with the bleeding shoulder slowed way down and I thought he was going to stop his car and get out, but he didn't, he just called me every name in the book. One guy threw an empty plastic bottle of spring water. I ignored everybody except that guy, who I flipped off riding with only one hand going in jerky wiggles over the narrow sidewalk. Pretty soon I was coasting downhill, squeezing the brake the whole time because I was afraid of gathering too much speed; the brake made a horrible, caged animal screech. I noticed how much debris there was on the sidewalk, and along the edge of the highway. There were hunks of concrete, big C-shaped shreds of tires, fast food bags, and flat cigarette butts. I felt the wind in my face. I bounced on the seat relaxing my shoulders and arms, pedaling backwards to make the *zzzzing* sound. At the bottom of the bridge I turned left onto East Bay, then rode along the park there and stopped to watch all the people and their children at the fountain. Every kind of kid in the whole world was there at the fountain. There were kids in shorts, kids in tennis shoes, kids in diapers, kids missing teeth, kids pretending to fly, kids crying, kids dancing standing right in the middle of the whole big erupting spray like this was some kind of celebration and they were going to soak in as much of it as they could. I began to feel uncomfortable with the stares I was getting from the sedentary, bored parents, so I moved on. I went over to the new pier, parked my bike and leaned over the railing to look at the mud down below. The tide was halfway out. The pungent, rotting sea smell was strong. I took in huge breaths that made me want to stretch out my arms and roar like a lion. I saw hundreds of mud crabs with their one big claw and one little claw, all of them eating mud. I lost track of time. I walked farther out and looked for the dark shadows of blue crabs in the shallow water. I found one, and watched him until I lost sight of him when he went out into deeper water. I got on my bike and rode past the fountain again and the children with their suspicious parents, toward the end of the Battery. I looked across the street to the pastel mansions and wrought iron gates. They looked hot sitting close to the street without much in the way of shrubbery around them. Men stood in tank tops or topless leaned over the railing that separated the Battery from the bay, their fishing poles leaned against the railing too, staring out into the white glare of the water, all sun-fried and hairy-chested and shameless. I looked in all the buckets as I went by. There's never much in the buckets and today wasn't any different. I stopped and talked to this guy, a friend of Reggie's that I went fishing with out in Reggie's boat. I told him who I was, but he didn't remember me too clearly. He had a huge blue crab in his bucket that he said he caught on his line.

"You didn't *hook* him?" I said.

"*Naaaaw*, he clawed the squid—wouldn't let go! Wouldn't let go all the way up until I netted him. . . Surprised the you-know-what outta me."

The crab was a beautiful turquoise blue in the claws. Reggie's friend taunted the crab with the handle end of the net. The crab snapped at it viciously in leaps that made the claws reach halfway up the side of the bucket.

"Can't believe he didn't let go," I said.

"Now he wished he would a!" The guy slapped his knee and

laughed like no tomorrow.

"Never seen anything like it," I told him.

"Live long enough and you'll see all kind of things. Heyuh-heyuh-heyuh."

"Shit, man; you got yourself one story to tell."

"This ain't nothin', boy. This ain't nothin' at all."

"Take it easy," I said, pushing myself off the side of the railing.

"Oh, I plan to."

I headed back toward the middle of the Battery. I rode past Jacque's, looking out the corner of my eye into the big pane window for Emily, but you couldn't see a thing because of all the reflections in the glass. I stopped in a corner grocery store and bought a big bottle of sweetened iced tea, and drank it in three breaths standing straddled over my bike in the partial shade of a rusted sign advertising bait and deli meat. When I was finished I walked on tiptoes over to a trashcan and threw the bottle away, and when I bent over to do it I felt all the cold iced tea in my empty stomach sloshing around. It was shortly after that when I began thinking about Carl. I was closer to the park than his bookshop, so I decided to see if he was there. The park, which is full of people during the week, was empty. The bright sun and sleepy air emphasized the emptiness and the whole scene made me depressed, like Sundays do, but it was only Saturday. Carl wasn't there. I headed toward the bookshop, but before I got there I passed this old bar with graffiti slashed all over the particle board front, and a small piece of paper that moved just barely in the nonexistent breeze that said *jazz music tonight*. I was afraid to park my bike, but I figured I'd only have one beer, and what were the odds that somebody'd steal it in the fifteen minutes I was in there? It was nice and cool inside with the air conditioner cranked up high. I sat down at the bar, which had soft black padding on it so you could put your forearms there in a natural position and never have them fall asleep. I had a beer without doing anything except look at the way the sun shined on the dull bar top, and how all the different colored booze in the different shaped bottles looked like an array of big jellybeans with the sun hitting them and reflecting in the big bar mirror. From where I was sitting I could see through the mostly boarded up window to Carl's place. I watched, and every so often somebody went in or came out. I couldn't help it, I kept thinking about my job. It's not that I couldn't find another job. In fact, I thought that losing that job just might end up being the best thing that ever happened to me. It was hard work and bad pay. You can get a job like that anywhere. Those jobs are for suckers, and I was tired of being a sucker. It got dark. Carl's place was closed. I didn't see him leave, but then I really wasn't paying attention. The bar was getting into high gear; the jazz band was setting up. I was real happy sitting there watching things happen. I loved being invisible. Everything was beautiful, and I thought things I hadn't thought of in years, and some I never had. My mind opened—there were no limits on where one thought ended and another began. I wanted to shoot to the stars, or swoop down on the ocean surface like a pelican and gulp it up. I left without saying bye to the bartender, and when I turned to look back at my spot at the bar it had already been swallowed up by people standing waiting for the band. The bike was still there. I headed back to the park.

The streetlights throbbed with moths. The air was tepid. I thought of tomorrow and Emily and the unknown. It's the unknown more than anything that keeps me going, and held me back from letting go of those big iron beams. I stopped the bike before the entrance, and leaned it against the wall. The sidewalk seemed wide in my drunkenness, and white like chalk. I walked slowly trying to be quiet. I could hear my steps echoing against the surrounding brick and stone buildings. I felt more like an intruder this time. I wasn't sure why I came back. I go to the beach fishing, I wander through the streets and alleys of town, I watch clouds and escape in them or realize answers to lifelong mysteries, and there's no reason I can give for doing any of them. I stood at the far end of the park, but I didn't sit down facing the bushes, or step onto the garden itself to crawl toward him. I sat down on the bench so that my back was to him. I wasn't afraid this time, or expectant. I didn't wonder if he was there; I made no attempt at dialogue with him. My intruder's guilt turned inward, and was lost in my reflective, mountain climber's high.

Life is a word, but the word means different things to different people. It means different things to Carl than it does to Reggie; it's one thing to Roxy and something totally different to Eddie; it's a completely different thing to Mike, Evelyn, Lyle, Antoinette, Tony, Lonnie, and me. We're such a small representation of the souls who experience life. There are billions of stories, most of them never told. I've often wondered how we might view it if the word *life* meant something more specific, more accurate. What if *life* was the Greek bastardization of *sacred sojourn*? What if it was the Chinese word for *perpetual change*? Or maybe the Mesopotamian root for the word meaning *unfulfilled dreams*? Would it make us view it any differently? I don't know about Shakespeare and his rose is still a rose by any other name comment; sometimes it is, and sometimes it's not. My own way has been made more difficult, I think, because I've had inaccurate pictures, at various times, of what life is. If you think I can tell you now what it is, I can tell you I can't. But, I think that because I've finally come to this realization, that I'll never feel comfortable *in* life, it's made me see it a little more clearly.

Something has happened to Carl; something so acutely profound, he sleeps alone in the park behind these bushes. For the longest time I've viewed it as a choice, a choice he freely makes. It may be. But, I don't believe it. I believe it's much more beyond his control than it is a choice. I didn't want to accept this idea months ago when it first began digging its roots in me. If I accepted it, then it meant I denied, at least somewhat, the concept of free will. And if I denied free will, then the idea of God and a natural order to things became more difficult to reconcile. And that lead me, of course, to the horrible possibility that life is not only unfair, but that there's nothing after it to even things out.

I want to go to Reggie's church, but I don't know what it would do for me. I want to join in the singing, and clapping, the celebration, the mourning, the brotherhood to which I do belong, but which I have an intense suspicion of. I'm afraid of being sucked in and losing the feel of pain, and joy. I don't want normalcy. I don't want sedation. I don't want to lose myself. I just want more of everything.

I understand pieces of Carl only slightly less than I understand pieces of myself, so that I can imagine the whole story. Who says I have to understand everything about him, or even me? It's in our nature to question, to reason, to categorize, to try and make sense of things. It may be that there is no sense, or if we find one, it may be nothing more than our own imagination or hope speaking, and not the great mirror to truth reflecting what we really are. But that's humanity; slipping on its belly from the sea of chaos, to run in herds of focused, confident stampedes, so it can return, winged, to the ocean-sky of chaos. It's not that poverty is beautiful, or disease, or suffering, or death; it's the struggle against it that's beautiful.

As I sat waiting, wondering, I thought of Emily. I pictured Alaska with its huge, clean waters. I imagined the two of us in a boat sailing between fjords of ice, among whales spouting high into the crystal blue sky.